The DragonFly Keeper

Tanya Pilumeli

FAVA PRESS

Cleveland, OH

Library of Congress Cataloging-in-Publication Data
Pilumeli, Tanya
The DragonFly Keeper / Tanya Pilumeli

Library of Congress Control Number: 2007909286

SUMMARY: Manuela and Silvia, two middle-grade sisters,
and their dog Fritz are recruited to travel the world to
save the DragonFly Keeper from the evil 'Rogs.'

ISBN 0-9801396-0-0

First Edition

Publisher's Cataloging-in-Publication
(Provided by Quality Books, Inc.)

Pilumeli, Tanya.
   The DragonFly Keeper / Tanya Pilumeli. — 1st ed.
   p. cm.
   SUMMARY: Manuela and Silvia, two middle-grade
sisters, and their dog Fritz are recruited to travel the
world to save the DragonFly Keeper from the evil "Rogs."
   LCCN 2007909286
   ISBN-13: 978-0-9801396-0-0
   ISBN-10: 0-9801396-0-0

   1. Middle school students—Juvenile fiction.
   2. Sisters—Juvenile fiction. 3. Magic—Juvenile fiction.
   4. Fantasy fiction. [1. Middle school students—Fiction.
   2. Sisters—Fiction. 3. Magic—Fiction. 8. Fantasy.]
   I. Title.

PZ7.P6317Dra 2008   [Fic]
                     QBI07-600319

For my mother
Jackie Grossner,
who gave me the precious gift of time

~ ~ ~

and in loving memory of my father
Warren Grossner,
(1936–2007)
whose spirit of determination
lives on within me.

Acknowledgments

The most thanks needs to be given to my mother, Jackie. Owning a restaurant with my husband and taking care of three kids ages 2, 3 and 5, I would never have written this book without her Saturday afternoon babysitting sessions. Of course, thanks to my nieces Manuela and Silvia who let me use them for this crazy adventure.

My father, Warren Grossner, always believed in me until his death in August, 2007. My husband, Alessandro, has believed in me during every crazy decision I have made. Thank you, Giuseppe, Violetta and Dionisio, for putting up with mama working on her book. Thanks to my uncle, Bob DeSan, Paula Elder, and Deb Bice for offering their proofreading skills and support. Sue Thomas tested the waters of *The DragonFly Keeper* on her class and gave me great ideas for classroom application. I owe thanks to my brother Mike Grossner and his wife Colleen and daughter Anna for letting me be obsessed with this project and for guidance. Thanks to Karena McCandless, Katie Reynolds, Sonja Seibert, Tatiana Parker, Marjorie Hallett. Thank you to Gale's Coffee Corner where the entire manuscript was written, and many glasses of green tea and delicious pastries consumed. Thank you to everyone at 1106 Design for a great interior and cover design. Thank you to all the many, many people who have helped me in so many ways to get this project out there. And thank you to God, for helping me achieve my dream.

Table of Contents

Chapter 1

Joining the Cause

"WHY DID YOU LET HIM OUT!" yelled Manuela as she tugged on her flip flops. "I don't see why I have to help you get him." She grabbed the leash and ran out the back door after Silvia who was already racing down North Barton, red flip flops flying and flapping.

Silvia hadn't meant to leave the door open, but she had forgotten her library books out on the picnic table and had only run out for a second. Of course, a second was all Fritz was waiting for, as her mother had reminded her angrily. She had looked up to see him streaking like a tan cheetah around the house and out down the sidewalk. Now Manuela was going to really rub it in that mom had made her help get him back. Big sisters.

Fritz was a fast dog and he loved this game. Silvia kept getting two feet away from him, and then, as he sat there panting, almost grinning, whoosh! He bounded away.

Finally, Manuela tip-toed up in front of Fritz, and Silvia slid in from behind. *We've got him now,* thought Silvia. Then Silvia stepped into a mud puddle and slipped bottom-first

1

into the muck. Fritz ran around the bushes towards a gated garden.

"Now what do we do?" Silvia asked, pushing back her curls. It had been a hot July day and the evening wasn't cooling off at all. She had just showered and put on pajamas, but by now was thoroughly miserable. "Should we go in there? I mean, it *is* getting dark."

"I have a better idea," Manuela said. She ran up to the rickety gate and slammed it shut. "Now all we have to do is ask whoever lives here to let us get Fritz, and we can go home. You owe me, Silvi."

Silvia looked through the fence. The light was getting dim; it was almost nine. She couldn't see much, but what she could see made her stomach tingle anxiously. What was supposed to be a garden was a chaotic tumble jumble of strange flowers, spiky weeds, gnarly trees and, in the middle, a giant peeling wooden pergola overrun with a big purple-leafed vine which ran throughout the entire garden. It could have been the dusk, but the house itself seemed darker and more disheveled than the surrounding houses. Small brown shutters covered all of the windows and the dark blue paint was smudgy and overshadowed by more of the mysterious purple vine. And where was Fritz? She couldn't even hear his panting and nothing moved in the stillness beyond the peeling white fence. "You go, Manu. I'm all wet."

"No, we both can go. You're the one who let him out anyway. We'll just ask if we can go around back. We don't have to go in. But let me talk, Silvi," Manuela said, turning toward the house. Silvia looked down. Her feet and flip-flops were all covered in damp, cut grass and she tried to rub off as much as she could. She rolled her eyes at Manuela's back as they walked slowly back around the bushes to the front of the house.

There was no front porch, only two concrete steps leading up to a landing with a twisted black iron hand rail. The windows were shuttered with ugly brown shutters here as well, and the bushes were so overgrown they practically engulfed the girls as they climbed the steps. There was so little space that Silvia had to stand behind Manuela as the older girl rapped on the door. After a few seconds, Manuela banged a little harder and then turned to go. "Come on, Silvi. No one lives here. Let's just go back there and get him."

But Silvia didn't move. She was staring at the glass pane in the middle of the door. Two golden eyes stared out at her. "Well, move, Silvi. I can't get down with you standing there. Let's go get him," Manuela said.

"Then you're going to have to go in *there* because, look!" Silvia pointed. Manuela turned around, and they saw Fritz's wagging tongue and goofy grin before he vanished inside. Silvia pushed Manuela aside and yanked open the door. "Come on, before he gets out again." Silvia whispered. Manuela bit her lip and frowned, her dark eyebrows lowering into a piercing glare. But Silvia smiled and turned back inside.

The first thing that hit her was the smell. It wasn't bad, just different. It was as if someone had spilled cinnamon and apple cider and had not bothered to clean it up. It was even darker inside, and when her eyes finally adjusted, Silvia saw a room overflowing with, well, things. She couldn't think of any other way of grouping the eccentric mish-mash arranged on an old table and dark, oily wooden floor and shelves all along the wall. Silvia started walking, dripping all over and making squishy sounds. Manuela caught her arm. "I can't believe you just walked in here. You can't just do that."

"Well Fritz did, and we need to get him out. Look at those bowls over there." Silvia said, shaking Manuela's hand off and squish-squashing over to the table. Her white T-shirt was mud-spattered and her blue boxers clung to her legs. But the bowls on the table fascinated her. There were dozens of them lined up in what seemed a random order. Silvia reached out to touch a particularly bright smooth pink bowl which looked like taffy when she saw movement out of the corner of her eye. Something softly swished past the partly opened door. She looked at Manuela and then slowly creaked open the door by pushing on its glass doorknob.

The smell intensified as the girls stepped into what Silvia soon realized was the kitchen. The floor was tiled in black and white and a lamp was turned on in the corner. Fritz sat there wagging his tail with his sloppy grin and next to him, with her back turned towards them, was a small hunch-backed woman. Her hair was gray and came out all over her head in curly cues. She wore a shapeless brown dress with a dark purple shawl around her shoulders. Curling up from the stove in front of her were wisps of steam which carried the strange smell over to the girls. "Hello, girls," she said without turning around. "I've been expecting you."

A few minutes later, the three of them were standing around a very small round table with a smooth, royal blue marble top. Even though it was a hot Cleveland summer night, and the windows were shut up, the house was cool. The girls were seated on top of pale blue kitchen towels to keep the wooden seats from getting wet. After some speechless hesitation, the old woman hobbled over smiling and put steaming mugs down on the table. Fritz followed her and stood next to her side when the woman stopped and looked up at Manuela and Silvia, for she was almost a foot shorter than even Silvia, who was tall for eight. "Girls," she said with a strange accent, "Fritz brought you to me, you know, now sit down and warm up, and I'll tell you everything."

"How did you know Fritz's name?" Silvia had her hands wrapped around her mug for she really was beginning to get cold now. She studied the gold flecks in the marble table top, but eventually looked up at the stranger.

"He told me, of course," the old woman said with a dry laugh. She winked at Silvia who wished she hadn't. The old woman's face wasn't so much wrinkled as it was full of crevices. Her skin was a smoky caramel color and her head seemed to pop up right out of her bosomy body. But Silvia couldn't look away from those eyes. They were the lightest blue she had ever seen. It was almost as if they were two glass portals misted over. She decided to believe the old lady right away.

"Oh, … kay. Well. Thank you for the, um, hot drink, but we have to get Fritz home. Our mom will be wondering where we are." Silvia felt Manuela kick her under the table, and she looked up to see the old lady winking again.

For the second time Silvia thought she glimpsed clouds roll by the woman's eyes when she did that. "Manu, I don't know why, but I believe her," she said, not taking her eyes away from the woman's face.

Silvia caught Manuela's glare, but looked away quickly. "Thank you, Silvia," the old woman said, and turned to Manuela. She reached out and placed her gnarled papery hand on Manuela's wrist. "Manuela, there is still time for you to believe, too. I need you both you know."

Manuela's mouth dropped open, but she didn't say anything. Silvia suppressed a smile. She could tell things were really not going the way Manuela had planned. "Alright. You know our names. Fritz seems to know you ..."

"And he likes her." Silvia said, rubbing the golden retriever's head affectionately. "Manu, let's just listen to her. She did help us get Fritz back after all." Silvia took a sip of her drink and sighed. Manuela rolled her eyes and then let out a huge sigh. Then she, too, drank from the fragrant appley-cinnamon drink. Silvia couldn't believe how wonderful the cider was. It was like a hot drinkable version of all her favorite desserts (and she had a lot of favorites) combined. The old woman's eyes were so entrancingly calm that, within a few minutes of silence, she felt that she had known her for a very long time. And she could see that Manuela was relaxing too. After all, as the elder girl at eleven, Manuela probably felt responsible for whatever happened. But Silvia knew that Manuela always liked a good adventure as much as she did, and this was turning out to be quite an adventure.

Soon the old woman broke the silence with her dry laugh. "I see you girls are ready to hear my story. A nice cup of sweet samudra always loosens up the magic in everyone." She scratched the end of her nose and then folded her knotty hands over her billowy bosom. "I am Miss Sasha Tingleroot, and you, my dears, are going to help save the magic in this sad world. For if the last of the magic DragonFlies are taken, and the DragonFly Keeper is not protected, well, then the world as we know it will no longer be.

"You see, people go to work; they cut their grass; they play football and soccer and talk on the phone. People go shopping or out to eat or stay in bed, and all along they think that it is their hard work, their government, their figures on paper which are keeping the neighborhood, the country, the planet together." Miss Sasha paused and took a sip of her own samudra. "But what only a few of us know, now you two included, is that it is the magic in us, in our minds, which keeps the world together. When a child picks a flower for her mother, the magic is blooming. When an artist has a vision of a cathedral, the magic is flowing. When a mathematician wakes up at two in the morning to finish his equation, the magic is churning. These things which make humans what they are, come from a special spice in the imagination which is the magic that is now threatened."

Miss Sasha got up from her chair and shuffled over to the cupboard. Reaching up as far as possible, she opened a smooth dark-paneled door and let out a quiet whistle. Suddenly a cat with the same smoky caramel coloring as Miss Sasha leapt up onto the counter and jumped into the cupboard. Fritz did a little half jog in place but sat down again when Silvia gripped his red collar. Then the cat jumped out again and dropped a little bag into Miss Sasha's hand. The old woman clasped the bag to her and shuffled back to the table. She didn't sit down again but, instead, leaned over the little table and placed the bag in the middle of the marble top. It was dark velvet green and was tied with an intricate black cord. She looked first at Silvia and then Manuela.

"What is that?" asked Manuela. She reached out to touch the bag, but Miss Sasha's hand shot out and caught her wrist.

"That is what you need to start your journey. But before I let you do that, I need to know you are committed. We don't have much time left," Miss Sasha said as she casually let go of Manuela and eased herself into her chair.

"But, committed to what? I still don't understand what is wrong, and what we have to do with it." Manuela said. "If you know so much about this magic, why do you even need us?"

"Fair enough question," said Miss Sasha with her dry laugh. "The younger we are, the more magic flows in our veins. It is just the way. Even though I am one of the few privileged older ones to still hold on to the belief in the DragonFly Keeper, I am not suited to take the journey as you two are. And, of course, Fritz."

"Fritz?" Silvia looked down at the now sleeping canine. "Fritz is going to help us?"

"Of course. He is an animal after all. Animals live within the magic naturally. Fritz will be a perfect helpmate along the way," said Miss Sasha. "And as for what is wrong, ah, well. For the answer to that, I need to know you believe enough to care." Miss Sasha took the girls' empty mugs to the sink and came back with some square buttery shortbread.

"Is this some magical cookie or something?" asked Silvia accepting the biscuit eagerly.

"No, dear, it is just shortbread. However, I do make good shortbread." Miss Sasha eased herself back into her chair and saw Manuela eyeing the green bag on the table. "So, are you two committed before I go any further? If you are worried about what your parents will think, don't. Time doesn't pass during this journey. When you are through, you can go home and tell your ma and pa all about it, but only a few minutes will have passed since you left your house."

Silvia looked at her watch. Already, a half an hour had passed.

"I want to save the magic." Silvia said calmly. She looked at Manuela and saw her smiling.

"Yes, Miss Sasha," Manuela said slowly. "I believe you can finish your tale. I am ready to help," and with that she grabbed a handful of shortbread cookies and settled back.

Chapter 2

The girls wear black hats

MISS SASHA CLOSED HER EYES and smiled a smile that seemed to bunch up the crevices in her cheeks into two boomerangs around her small nose. "Ah girls, I am so pleased," she said. "Now I can tell you all you need to know. But we must hurry. The DragonFly Keeper must be found."

"I still don't see how two girls and a dog are going to save this DragonFly Keeper," Manuela said. "And we are wearing our pajamas. We can't possibly get up and go now."

Miss Sasha pointed a gnarly finger at Manuela. "Listen first, then ask as many questions as you need," she said without opening her eyes. "I don't want any interruptions either. Save the questions until I am through."

Silvia had been studying the table top. After staring at the velvet green bag she began to gaze at the marble. She found the gold swirls in the blue marble hypnotic. She began tracing them with her finger and suddenly realized they looked like little flies. Like dragonflies, she thought.

She looked up to see Miss Sasha's hypnotic eyes on her. "DragonFlies," Silvia said softly.

"Yes. I am a special custodian of the magic. I am nothing like the DragonFlies and the Keeper, but I have my uses. You see, I am old. Very, very old. Someone as old as me is put in charge of certain secrets. The DragonFlies that carry the magic throughout the world are immune to most problems: floods, fires, any natural disaster. The only enemy they have is Shatru." Miss Sasha took a deep breath and closed her eyes again. "He has always tried to take the magic from the DragonFlies and the Keeper for many, many thousands of years. But he has never before captured the Keeper."

"Why don't the DragonFlies rescue him themselves?" Silvia asked leaning forward.

"Well, my dear," Miss Sasha said, "they don't know where he is being held. You see, Shatru was originally a balancer. He was permitted in the world to keep people from forgetting how important the magic was. Wherever Shatru has been, his influence produces sadness, despair and desperation." She opened her eyes and the boomerangs around her mouth dipped as she frowned. "But the world is now so full of sadness, despair and desperation, and this gives Shatru power. He has used that power to capture the Keeper.

"The DragonFly Keeper descends from a direct line of very powerful DragonFlies. His role is to oversee the spread of the magic. He controls the magic, you see. What Shatru wants is that control. If he gets it, well, let's just say that would be very, very bad." Miss Sasha coughed a dry raspy cough and shuffled in her apron pocket until she pulled out a small blue glass vial with an ornate gold stopper. She pulled out the stopper and took a tiny sip and then replaced the top. She closed her eyes as she replaced the vial within the folds of her apron.

"A Keeper once placed some reserve magic in a special place long ago. But Jiwan, the Keeper, and his daughter, Hira, do not even know where. If Shatru gets this reserve, he can gain control of all the magic. But, even if he does not get this, he will slowly destroy the Keeper and drain all of the magic from the world."

Manuela began to fidget with a question, but Silvia opened her eyes really wide and gave her a warning stare. She had thought of a question, probably the same one. *Where was this magic, and is that how they would save the Keeper?* But that would have to wait until Miss Sasha Tingleroot had finished.

"You girls are still young enough to communicate with those who live in the magic realm. With the right tools, and, yes, clothes, certain individuals in contact with the DragonFly world will be able to find you and send you in the right direction. I have those tools. Now, before we get you ready for the journey, any questions?" Miss Sasha opened her eyes only slightly.

Manuela shot a swift glance at Silvia and asked, "How exactly are we to make this grand rescue? Is there a formula? A map? A genie in a lamp?"

"What Manu means, Miss Sasha," Silvia kicked Manuela under the table, "is that we've never actually saved anyone before. What are our instructions?"

Miss Sasha reached out and grabbed the green bag and then got up from the table slowly and began to waddle into the first room the girls had entered. When she got to the doorway she stopped and looked back. "Well, I don't actually know what you are going to do, but you will know what to do when it is time. Now let me get your things." And with that she hobbled into the darkness.

After only a few minutes in which Manuela and Silvia munched the last of the shortbread in a heavy silence, Miss Sasha returned to the doorway and motioned for them to follow her. Fritz stretched and yawned and then trotted through the doorway with the girls close behind.

Near the far end of the room, Miss Sasha stood waiting next to some clothing laid out on the floor. Silvia cocked her head a little as she tried to understand the costumes. Each outfit had a poofy layered skirt made out of stiff cotton. The smaller one was a bright blue and the other an olive green. Two fuschia sweaters and about four white T-shirts were laid out next to them. Finally, there were two blue and gold woven blankets. But by far the strangest part of the get-up were the two black derby hats stacked on top. Silvia shrugged at Manuela, and then they both started to change.

While they put on the layers of clothing, Miss Sasha sat in a little wooden chair. "These clothes are for the first leg of the journey. You will get there with this." She held out the little green velvet bag, swinging it by the black cord.

"So where are we going? To a Halloween party?" Manuela raised an eyebrow and half-smiled. Miss Sasha made her boomerang smile and pulled the bag back down into her lap.

"Ah, yes. The hats do make for an interesting outfit. I suppose anywhere else you would look out of place. But not in the Andes mountains of Bolivia." Miss Sasha said. Manuela's smile faded. Silvia popped her head through her sweater and gasped.

"Mountains? Bolivia?" Silvia was really excited now. She had always wanted to travel. "But, isn't that really far away? Like in Africa?"

Miss Sasha was fingering the little bag, rolling it back and forth between her rough hands. "South America. And it is far, but only if you don't have this." Opening the bag, Miss Sasha delicately dropped its contents into the palm of her right hand. It was a blue pebble with gold speckles. As Miss Sasha held out her palm, the low light from the one floor lamp reflected its smooth, shiny surface.

Silvia waited, knowing by now that Miss Sasha would explain. "This, my dears, is a *shaanti* or place-stone. If you have the right words, you can use it to move from place to place in an instant. I have the words to take you to Kalahuta, an island in Lake Titicaca on the northwestern border between Bolivia and Peru. But that's all I have. After that you must find the Weaver. He is your contact." Miss Sasha took Silvia's right hand and placed the pebble in her palm. It was cool and heavier than it looked.

Looking into each girl's eyes in turn, she said, "You must follow three rules in using a *shaanti*. First, you must always enclose it in your right palm. Secondly, you must hold any other travelers with your left hand and form a chain." Here Miss Sasha paused and closed Silvia's fingers tightly around the stone. Then she brought Manuela's right hand over and placed it on top of Silvia's. "Finally, you must never, ever lose it."

With the stone back in the green velvet bag and the bag tightly secured and in her blue skirt pocket, Silvia used an old mirror to tie back her curly brown hair with a black string. She looked at Manuela in the foggy mirror doing the same. There had been a brief spat in which they had argued over who would carry the *shaanti*. Manuela had insisted that she was by far more responsible, while Silvia had known that she earned the right to carry it by entering Miss Sasha's house in the first place. Miss Sasha had only laughed her dry raspy laugh and caressed Fritz during the episode. Finally she suggested the girls take turns, with Silvia having the first turn since she did come in first. Manuela had grudgingly conceded, worrying out loud if she would ever get her turn, or if Silvia would loose the *shaanti* first. Miss Sasha's laugh cut short at this and she abruptly stood up which silenced the girls immediately. On no circumstance should they joke about loosing the *shaanti* or about the journey, she had said. It was then that she told them that it could be dangerous as well.

"Shatru's Rogs will be watching for you. The Rogs will try to stop you any way they can. Do you understand?" Of course she didn't. Silvia looked at herself in the cloudy mirror, adjusting the silly hat. What was she doing? She hadn't even *heard* of Bolivia before, and here she was going with only Manuela and Fritz. While she wanted to believe in Miss Sasha, the whole thing was very bizarre and secretly she was waiting for the chance to use the *shaanti* to solidify the story.

Her round face looked pale in the low light. She was tall for eight, and strong. Her brown eyes hid under long lashes in the shadowy light, and her ears were clearly defined with her hair back. Silvia always knew her expressions made her look like she was always concentrating, but the derby hat made her look like some kooky magician.

Manuela stood next to her adjusting her clothes. She was also tall with long dark curly hair. But her face was longer and oval and a deeper color. Her hair was so thick, that even tied back it billowed out around her cheeks and from under the hat. *If I look like a magician*, thought Silvia wryly, *then Manu looks like a musician. She just needs a guitar.* Her thoughts were interrupted by Fritz who snuggled into her legs.

The skirts reached to just below the knee, and Miss Sasha had said that the flip flops would have to go. She had left for a minute while the girls were adjusting their hats. When Silvia looked up from Fritz, Miss Sasha was coming through the door carrying two backpacks over her arm and holding two pairs of clunky brown boots. "In these bags you will find some useful traveling items," she said. She dropped the boots to the floor with a thud. "You will need these to keep your feet warm, dry and protected. Lake Titicaca is warm during the day, but at night it can get very cold." *At night?* Silvia shivered.

"How will we find the Weaver you mentioned? What does he look like?" Manuela asked as she pulled on the thick wooly socks Miss Sasha handed them. They were sitting on the floor with Fritz between them.

Miss Sasha was sitting in the little wooden chair again. She sighed. "I've told you all I know. When it is time to leave, I will give you the words for the *shaanti*, but the task at hand is now yours. I wish I could help more; I would love to go with you." Miss Sasha coughed slightly and then reached into her pocket for her blue vial. After a sip, she sighed again. "I am old. I cannot make this journey with you. But you were chosen for this, so do not be afraid."

She leaned forward after placing her vial in her apron. The girls stopped lugging on the boots as Miss Sasha grabbed their wrists. "Believe in yourselves, trust each other, and always keep going." Her water-colored eyes danced in the shadows and her mouth slowly twitched into a smile as she let go and rocked back up into the chair.

Silvia stood up, and with Fritz circling them excitedly, they followed Miss Sasha back into the kitchen. The boots made a heavy clunky sound on the boards of the dark living room. As they passed the table once again, Silvia stopped to look at the bowls. "Miss Sasha," she said. "Can I ask you what all these bowls are for?"

"My bowls?" Miss Sasha looked back through the doorway. "Oh yes, those are gifts from friends. I collect hand-made bowls, you see. Each bowl tells me a story of its giver and how it was acquired. Come now, it is time." She turned and continued through to the kitchen.

The girls followed with their backpacks on, stuffed with the traveling items and the woven blankets. In the kitchen the appley-cinnamon smell was strong again, and Miss Sasha walked over to the stove to fill two mugs with samudra. "This will give you strength and warmth to start your journey," she said as she handed each of them a mug. "And for you too!" she smiled as she put a bowl of the warm drink on the floor for Fritz who lapped it up eagerly.

After gulping down the samudra, the girls felt excited and full. Miss Sasha opened a door in the corner of the room which led out into the backyard. "Into the garden we go, and don't trip on my vine, please." Miss Sasha disappeared into the darkness.

Manuela grabbed Silvia's hand as Fritz dashed out the door and down some steps. "Are you sure we should be

doing this, Silvi? What if ... What if we don't come back?"
Her eyebrows bunched together in a frown.

"Manu," Silvia said smiling. "*I* believe we will. Besides,
if what Miss Sasha says is true, then we have nothing to
lose. If we don't save the Keeper, no one will. What will
the world be like then?" She squeezed Manuela's hand
and felt her reluctantly squeeze back. Silvia let go and
turned toward the dark door. She was afraid, too. But her
curiousness always got the better of her. She walked into
the garden feeling the warm, humid air hit her like a puff
of breath.

The stairs were squeaky wooden boards with another
twisted iron railing. It was so dark that she could barely
see the ground to put her boot down. At first she couldn't
see anything but overgrown vegetation, but finally she saw
Fritz's tail swishing ahead and off to the right and heard
him bark. She fumbled over the broken stone pathway, feeling the skirt for the bulge of the *shaanti* in her pocket. They
finally reached Miss Sasha and Fritz who were standing
by the crazy-looking pergola. Even in the darkness, Silvia
could make out the big purple-leafed vine winding around
the supports and roof of the pergola. Up close, she could see
that the paint was originally a pale blue, but it was peeled
off in most places. Miss Sasha motioned for them to climb
up the pergola's steps and enter the tomb-like interior.

"Please go on up, I will follow you to wish you farewell
and to give you the words you need to begin your journey."
Miss Sasha motioned again towards the dark hollow at the
top of the rickety stairs. The night was full of summertime
smells. It had been a very rainy summer in Cleveland and
the fecund smell of thick vegetation was exhaling in the
night air. The air was still damp from the earlier rain and

the crickets were still going strong. As she climbed the steps slowly, Silvia thought she could smell a faint apple smell coming from the giant purple leaves twined around the pergola. The leaves fanned out from the vine in rounded triangles and were as big as elephant ears.

Inside the pergola, it was so dark that it was hard to see beyond a few feet from the entrance. Silvia pulled out the *shaanti* and held it tightly in her right palm. Miss Sasha put her hands on the girls' shoulders and smiled her smile. Her face was so creviced in the shadows that Silvia began wondering how old Miss Sasha really was. Her intense watery eyes looked ghostly in the pale moonlight entering through the leaves on the pergola. Silvia shivered involuntarily and took a step closer to Manuela who grasped her left hand reassuringly. Manuela reached down and grabbed Fritz's red collar firmly in her left hand.

Miss Sasha winked down at Fritz and then looked back up at the girls with a more serious air. "This journey will test your strength. You will feel alone and helpless and want to give up." Then Miss Sasha reached out and took each girl by the wrist. "Remember to rely on each other. Only by working together can you free the DragonFly Keeper. You *must* not give up. I am not sorry to bring you girls into this. I believe in both of you, and now you must believe in each other and yourselves." She lowered her hands to her sides.

"Before I give you the words for the *shaanti*, I have another gift." Reaching into an unseen pocket of her brown dress, Miss Sasha brought out a necklace. Dangling from a red velvet ribbon, an intricately decorated gold circle the size of a quarter glinted in the darkness. When Miss Sasha held it up to the pale shaft of moonlight that was coming in through the pergola, Silvia saw that it was inlaid with deep green emeralds, midnight blue sapphires, and flaming pink and soft lavender stones. "As the younger, I place this Newari Gau Locket on you, Silvia. It is my parting gift. You can place your prayers inside. Keep it close to your heart."

Silvia didn't know what to say. She felt Manuela's eyes on her and didn't look up. "You must close your eyes, and then, Silvia, you alone must repeat the words three times out loud because you hold the *shaanti*." Silvia closed her eyes immediately, grateful not to have to look at Manuela's disappointed face. "This will only work to get you to Kalahuta. The Weaver will tell you words that will take you to your next destination. Each contact will give the instructions you need to complete your journey. However, you two must make the critical decisions together that will lead you to the DragonFly Keeper." Silvia heard her shuffle off a bit, and then Miss Sasha spoke softly. "I wish you strength and hope that I have been able to prepare you."

Silvia squeezed the *shaanti* tightly. Manuela squeezed her hand and they waited. "This is in the Aymara language, a pre-Incan language that was spoken at Lake Titicaca and is still spoken by people today. *Sajuna Paqu, sara. Ikiw puritu. Kalahuta.* It means 'Blue-gilded one, I go away. I am with dream. Kalahuta.' I will repeat it several times. Please say it in your head until you are *sure* that you have it right, Silvia. Then nod so that I know that you are ready." Miss Sasha began repeating the strange mantra slowly in a soft voice.

Silvia began to shiver again as she tried to concentrate on the strange sounds. *Sajuna Paqu, sara.* Blue-gilded one, I go away. *Ikiw puritu. Kalahuta.* I am with dream. Kalahuta.

She felt Manuela's hand surely in hers and took a deep breath. Finally, after hearing the chant for a few minutes, Silvia felt the moment. She nodded slightly and Miss Sasha stopped. Squeezing Manuela's hand she took a deep breath. *"Sajuna Paqu, sara. Ikiw puritu. Kalahuta."*

Chapter 3

Kalahuta

RIGHT AWAY MANUELA OPENED HER EYES. She knew that she was supposed to keep them closed, but her body was shocked into opening them. From the silent feel of the pergola and its soft dewy night smell, the air had gone dry and was whipping her hair around. She had instinctively reached up for her hat, letting go of Fritz's collar. What she saw made her mouth drop open, which wasn't a good idea because the wind was dusty and immediately made her mouth feel gritty.

"Manu! It really worked! We are *definitely* not in Cleveland, Ohio." Silvia let go of Manuela's hand to hold her hat as well. Fritz hunched down between them with a little whine.

Manuela couldn't respond. Her mouth closed now, she kept her eyes fixed on the scene around her. Gone was the quiet darkness of the vine-covered pergola. Before her was a vast lake about fifty yards away down a steep incline. Steel-grey peaked water was splashing the shore and spraying high up into the air. The lake was eerie in the pre-dawn light. Above it in the distance, a magnificent range of snow-capped mountains glowed a faint red-gold from the early sun. Manuela had never seen mountains like these before; she hadn't even seen much of a big hill for that matter. The air was cool, and she grabbed Silvia's hand and pulled her to the side where there was a clump of rocks and an area of sheltering pine trees.

"I really didn't think it would happen, Silvia. I mean, I *wanted* it to happen, but how could it happen?" Manuela kept rubbing her forehead and then stealing glances ahead at the lake.

"Well, it happened," Silvia said. She looked excited but fearful. Manuela knew she had to get a grip on herself if they were going to get over the shock of being thrown into this strange land.

"We must be in Bolivia. This looks like it could be Lake Titicaca, and see there," Manuela pointed ahead to some dark splotches she saw on the lake, "those could be islands. We should wait until there is more light, and then we can figure out what to do."

"We need to get to Kalahuta." Silvia said as she sat down next to the rocky base of one of the trees.

"I know that. But we haven't even looked in these packs yet. And with the wind and the little light, we are going to fall on our butts if we try to walk anywhere." She sat down next to Silvia and unbuckled her pack. It was old and used-looking. The tan canvas sack had a large flap which buckled low on the pack in two places. The simple shoulder straps also had adjustable buckles.

Silvia quickly turned her attention from the far mountains to her own canvas pack and the girls pulled out the rolled blankets which they had stuffed in before they left.

"I'm glad Miss Sasha thought of these," Silvia said. She threw hers around her shoulders before returning back to the pack. Manuela placed hers on the ground rolled up. The bright blue and gold weaves of Silvia's blanket looked cheery in the dim setting. Manuela smiled as she saw her sister's hair spiraling out around her like some strange sea anemone in the wind.

The rest of the items in the pack were small. On top was a small, thin black flashlight, which Manuela turned on so as to see the contents better. Soon she saw a similar light near Silvia's pack. She saw a canteen full of water, a compass, a tiny flute, a map of the Lake Titicaca region, a long piece of cord wound up, a conch shell the size of a fist, an empty blue velvet bag, and a small bag of Miss Sasha's shortbread cookies.

"I have a little red bowl!" Silvia said excitedly, passing the small clay bowl to Manuela. The rest of Silvia's things were similar to Manuela's except that she didn't have a flute or a shell. Silvia also had an orange velvet bag and a black plastic lei like the colorful ones used at luaus. "Why is this plastic lei black? And why in the world would Miss Sasha stick this in my pack?" Silvia wondered out loud.

"Well, she must know something we don't yet. I suggest we look at the map and then try to sleep a little." Manuela said, giving the black lei back to Silvia.

"I'm going to eat these cookies. They really are pretty good." Silvia said. She opened her pack and picked one out, chomping into it with vigor.

"If I were you, I'd save them until we are really hungry. We don't know when or what we will be eating next, Silvi," Manuela said as she grabbed the bag out of her sister's hands before she could devour the whole thing.

"Hey, I'm hungry now, thank you. You don't have to tell me *everything* to do, you know. I'm sure we will find something when we need it." Silvia grabbed the bag back and glared at Manuela.

Suit yourself, Manuela thought. *Just don't ask for mine later on.* If it was one thing that she couldn't stand, it was when she was right and then she still had to pay for it in the end. She spread the map out in front of them. It wiggled too much in the wind until they anchored the corners with their packs. "By the way, Silvi, maybe you should give me the *shaanti* now. It will be my turn next anyway, and this way we won't loose it."

Silvia looked around her and then scooped up the small stone, which she had laid down on the moss next to her. Instantly she gave a defensive scowl and slipped the *shaanti* in the pocket of her skirt. "Why do you always have to sound like you know everything? I can handle things fine myself."

Manuela let out a sigh of exasperation. All she needed right now was Silvia to get all huffy. At least she knew the *shaanti* was safe for the moment. She smoothed out the map in front of her and then traced the lake with her finger. "This says that our island is in the middle part of the lake. But where are we?" She pulled out her compass and watched it swivel around. "Silvi, shine your light on this."

Silvia swung her flashlight towards the compass, and they both watched the dial. "It looks like the lake lies *south* of us. But where exactly are we on the north shore?" Manuela put the compass back in her pack.

"You mean you can't figure something out? I'm surprised," Silvia remarked sarcastically as she finished off the last cookie and stuffed the empty bag in her pack. Manuela ignored her. "Well, I guess we will have to go down to the lake to see better. I can't see anything from here except those mountains." Silvia began to get up.

"Wait, Silvia. We'll wait until there is more light. I told you it might be dangerous." Manuela reached out and laid her hand on Silvia's arm. Silvia shook it off and grabbed her pack. She stood up and pulled the blanket around her closer.

"Let me just tell *you* something, Miss Manuela. *I* am the one who got us here in the first place. If it weren't for me, we would be home watching re-runs of *SpongeBob*. So, I am going to go down there and get a closer look if I think it is a good idea." Before Manuela could get to her feet, Silvia had turned and sprinted off in the semi-light.

"Silvi! Wait! We shouldn't split up! What if you get lost?" Manuela threw the rest of her stuff in her pack and grabbed her blanket. But by the time she got out from the clump of trees, Silvia was nowhere to be seen. Fritz had been lying quietly until Manuela's burst of shouting, and now he was pacing back and forth confused.

Manuela didn't know what to do. Not only were they separated, Silvia had the *shaanti*. How were they to accomplish anything if they couldn't even stick together to find the first contact. She took a couple of deep breaths. *She said she was going to the shore*, thought Manuela. *She couldn't have gone that far yet. Fritz can find her.* Dawn was brighter, but the wind had picked up as well. Manuela held on to her hat and crouched down next to Fritz.

"Fritz, we need to find Silvia. Got that, boy? Find Silvi. Go," she told him. Fritz went a few paces then came back whining, then went a few paces again. Finally he stopped and looked back at Manuela. She sighed. He was right. It was hard to even breathe in this dust, and Manuela could barely even make out the tree clump a few yards behind her. Patting her leg, she called Fritz back and slowly walked back to the shelter of the trees with her hand covering her face. When she got there, she sat down and pulled her blanket around her. She cradled Fritz's head in her lap. "I'm sure Silvia will see how dangerous it is. I'm sure she will come right back. You'll see, Fritz," Manuela said soothingly to the dog. *Please, Silvi. Don't leave me here*, she thought as she brushed away a lone tear.

Coughing, Silvia stumbled down farther. After the first few minutes she knew Manuela had been right, but she wasn't going to go back up until she had her look. *For principle's sake*, she thought. The pack was bumping against her leg as she tripped over rocks and stumbled on the uneven ground. When her cough got worse she crouched down and put the blanket over her head. After a minute she opened the blanket enough to peek out. *Which way was the lake?*

All she could see was a gritty gray. And the smell! It smelled like rotten tomatoes. Curling up, Silvia fought the urge to cry. She thought of Manuela and Fritz and how she had just run off without thinking. But she couldn't find them now. Pushing her fists into her eyes, she tried not to listen to the howl of the wind, and soon she was fast asleep.

Chapter 4

Waking up to a dream

SILVIA GRUMBLED. Her hair was soaked with sweat, and she didn't know why she was stuck under her blanket. And why was she on the ground? Groaning she found her way out from under the covers and opened her eyes. At first her mouth dropped open in shock. "It wasn't a dream," she said finally to no one. Before her was Lake Titicaca drenched in a spectacular sprinkle of sunshine. The waves lapped lazily against the shore a few yards from where she sat. A few birds which looked like black ducks with flame-orange tips waddled up into a clump of reeds. While there was still a rotting sort of smell lingering, other sweeter smells mingled with it. Some large red flowers she had flattened while she slept, for example, which reminded her of a spicy honeysuckle.

Stiffly, she got up and looked down at her skirt. The blue was more like khaki brown now. Her bright purple sweater was caked in dust, and she could only imagine that her face and hair were a big clump. *It is so hot,* she thought. *What a strange place.* Donning her funny hat, she slowly made her way down to the shore, easily avoiding the rocks, potholes and stiff reed clumps which had so confused her in the dust-storm. After setting her pack down on some golden grass, she took off her boots, socks and sweater. At least the T-shirt she unveiled was clean. Big birds swooped over the lake. Behind her, birds cackled in the trees sounding out the morning. Nimbly she put her left toes in and sighed. *Ahh. This is better.* She waded right in up to her knees, holding up the dusty skirt.

Ahead on the horizon, the mountains glowed a warm orange as the sun slanted in from her left. *It must still be early morning, but that sun is so bright!* Wading back to the shore she splashed her face and supped some water from her palms. Looking up the bank she thought of Manuela and Fritz. *I guess I should have waited. Well, at least I did get the first look,* Silvia thought as she put her socks and boots back on. Stuffing her sweater in the pack, she started trudging up the slope. But every sparse group of tree clumps looked alike. "Manu! Fritz! It's me, Silvi! Manu! Wake up!"

Off to her left, Silvia thought she saw something moving behind a bigger gnarly-looking pine tree. "Manu? Is that you? Answer me!" Silvia yelled into the distance. Now she was angry. Just because she had gone off last night, shouldn't be a reason for Manuela to begin ignoring her. *Well, Miss Sasha told us to stay together. I guess I better tell her I'm sorry for running off. But she had better apologize for being bossy.* As she walked toward the gnarly tree, she noticed that more and more of the trees were covered with a draping Spanish moss. "Manu? Please answer now," Silvia pleaded with apprehension in her voice.

Finally, she reached the tree and looked around. Little purple flowers were all around the base of the tree. The breeze was a little warmer here, and the rotting smell from the lake was not as strong. Manuela and Fritz were nowhere in sight. Silvia sat down and remembered she was hungry. Rummaging in her backpack she pulled out her empty bag of shortbread cookies and frowned. She looked down at the beautiful range of mountains at the far side of the lake. Their majestic slopes changed from purple to pink as the sun peaked over the mountains in the east. *This place does feel magical. I wonder how we will ever find our way out of here.* Apprehensively, Silvia palmed the pocket with the *shaanti* in it, relaxing slightly as she felt the familiar bump.

Putting the empty bag back in her sack, she drained her canteen and began looking around to try to find Manuela and Fritz. Suddenly she got up and threw her pack over her shoulders. Further up the slope she could see a ridge with a dark opening in it. *A cave! Manuela and Fritz must have seen it too!* She ran over the rocky ground as best she could in her clunky boots. Reaching the cave entrance, she bent over and pushed her way in.

Automatically Silvia knew something was wrong. Her feet started sliding out from under her and her arms splayed out to try to grab hold of something. But she only brushed away crumbling stone and dirt. She felt the air rush out of her lungs as her back hit the ground with only her pack for cushioning. Then, without being able to scream, Silvia felt herself sliding and then tumbling far, far down into the mountains.

Manuela turned her face and buried it into her arms to keep Fritz from licking her cheeks, but then he just started slobbering her ears, which was by far worse. "Fritz, cut it out. Yuck, Fritz, stop it." Manuela rolled over and sat up rubbing her eyes. Sunlight poured in through the tree branches and the sounds of strange birds made her remember where she was. *Silvia!* She thought. *That stubborn girl. She's always doing things without thinking.* Manuela opened her pack and found her water. She poured some for Fritz in a little tree root hollow and then finished off the rest. The dusty storm had made her feel sticky and gritty, but she figured she could wash up at the lake where she would hopefully find Silvia. Gathering her hat and other things and stuffing her sweater into her pack, Manuela started down the slope with Fritz sniffing around at everything.

In the daylight Manuela could see that the slopes were very rocky and covered in a red-green grass that seemed to shimmer. As she approached the shore of the lake, she stopped, covering her nose instinctively. "Whoa, that is *not* what I was expecting. Fritz, what do you think of that stink?" Manuela watched as Fritz gingerly stuck his nose in the air near the water. Then he cautiously approached the lake and began lapping it up.

"Well, I guess it could be worse," Manuela sighed and took off her boots and socks.

After cleaning up and refilling her canteen, Manuela began walking along the shore. She couldn't believe Silvia wasn't there. *She couldn't have wandered off too far,* Manuela thought. *Why didn't she come back?* Suddenly Fritz began barking and jumping all around. He was sniffing at a clump of reeds and grass a few yards ahead of her. Manuela raced ahead and looked at what had Fritz so excited. There on the ground, among some muddy boot prints, lay a compass *exactly like Manuela's.* "These have to be Silvi's, Fritz!" Manuela grabbed it and then looked around. The sun was higher now and the sky was a giant blue tent stretched from mountain to mountain. But there was no sign of Silvia.

"Fritz, can you sniff out where she went?" Manuela asked the dog, rubbing his neck and pointing to the few muddy prints. Fritz barked and seemed to understand. He started circling around and then paused. Barking again, he trotted up the slope towards a giant pine tree. Manuela struggled to keep up with him, stashing the compass in her skirt pocket. "That Silvia," she grumbled, "why couldn't she just stay put and wait for me to find her? We are never going to find Kalahuta and our contact this way."

Adjusting her pack, Manuela reached the giant tree and saw Fritz trotting towards a low ridge. "Fritz, wait! I can't keep up with you!" Manuela took a deep breath and trudged on. Fritz had stopped at the ridge and was barking at it. When she got closer, Manuela could see it was some sort of cave or hole. She threw down her pack and ran over to the hole and looked inside. Beyond it was very dark and steep. "Silvia! Silvia! Are you in there? Silvia! Answer me!" Fritz lay down with his nose near the hole and whined. Manuela remembered her flashlight and ran back to get her pack. She shone the light into the hole, but could only see a never-ending rockslide. "Silvia, say something!" Manuela lay down next to Fritz and stared down the hole at the darkness. What was she supposed to do now?

For a few seconds, Silvia felt she was floating. She couldn't tell if she were lying down or up, or whether she had her eyes opened or closed. Her body ached and she heard a train rumbling around her head. Finally, sensation came back, and she felt the cool stones under her and cautiously tried to move. The darkness was so total; she couldn't even see when she put her hand right in front of her eyes. The sensation was eerie. She knew her eyes were open, yet it was as if she were blind. Slowly she sat up and realized she was lucky she had not been injured too badly. Scooting around she felt her pack and then tried to reach around for a wall. Not finding any she kept inching along until she remembered the flashlight.

It seemed to take her forever to feel around the pack and find the little flashlight. Silvia flicked it on. At first the brightness made her squint, but then she adjusted to the light and looked around. She gasped. She was inside a fairly big underground cavern. The walls sparkled with a silvery glow wherever she shone her flashlight, and all around the outer wall were holes of varying sizes, one which trickled a little water. Her funny little hat lay beat-up in the middle of the cavern.

She passed the flashlight back and forth trying to find the hole from which she emerged. Finally, she started shaking and dropped the flashlight in her lap. Covering her face with her hands she bent over and felt her stomach get tight as she stifled a sob. *Please let this all be a dream. Please. Please. What am I doing here? Why did I think I was special? Manu, where are you?* Silvia rocked back and forth letting tears silently fall into her palms.

Finally, her grumbling stomach brought her to reality. Wiping her eyes, she took a deep breath and picked up the flashlight. She knew she had no more food and had foolishly drunk up all her water without refilling her canteen at the lake. Tentatively, she stood up, shouldered her pack, and walked over to the nearest wall to look at the holes.

Some were obviously too small. However, there were at least five from which she could have slipped out. Silvia shuddered and tried not to be paranoid about the darkness and the empty holes around her. Slowly she put her face near each of the larger holes in the nearest wall. They all seemed the same.

Working her way around the wall, Silvia kept checking out the holes. She thought she heard some soft scratching and turned around abruptly shining the light all around. All she could see were shimmering stones and dark holes. Slowly she turned back around and put her face in front of the next hole. It was fairly big, and Silvia flashed her light up into it. Then she blinked in surprise. There was a *breeze* coming from this hole. It was very faint, but she felt it for sure. And then she heard what she thought was Manuela calling her name. Excitedly, she decided that this was her way out. Trying to shine the light in farther, however, she saw that the hole curved up almost vertically. She bit her lip and tried not to yell. That is when she heard the scratching again, louder this time and directly behind her. It was distinctly the scrabbling of stones. Silvia felt the hair on her neck raise and her heart jumped inside her. She was frozen. If she turned around, she would see what it was and most certainly not like it. If she didn't turn around, she wouldn't be able to see what was crawling up behind her, and that seemed worse.

Very quickly Silvia spun around, slamming her back into the cave wall to the right of the hole. She held her flashlight in front of her like a gun and screamed. Not two feet in front of her sat a very big, very black, very red-eyed rat.

It seemed like Manuela had been yelling down the hole a long time before she thought she heard a scream. With a start, she and Fritz both leaned forward listening. But the only sounds she could hear were from the wild ducks flying by. "I have an idea, Fritz," Manuela turned to her backpack and rummaged inside, finally pulling out the length of cord. "Maybe if I tied this around you, you could reach Silvia. Then I could pull the two of you out." Manuela started winding the cord around Fritz's back and under his front legs. He didn't look too happy about it.

When Manuela was finished, she coaxed Fritz over to the hole. When he didn't go in right away she tried pushing him and yelling Silvia's name at him. But Fritz would have none of it. He firmly planted his legs and leaned away from the hole. Finally, Manuela collapsed in tears. This was not some fairytale at all. They hadn't even begun their journey and already danger had found them. She pressed the heels of her palms into her eyes and sighed.

"Kamisaraki," said a smooth deep voice behind her. Manuela jumped up and twirled around grabbing her hat as it fell off. Now, Manuela knew that she was in a far away place, having got there by a magic stone, and that she was wearing the strangest outfit she ever saw. However, she was not prepared for the small smooth-faced man who stood there with a big grin on his face. He was shorter than Manuela and very wiry. Wrapped around his body was a bright blue and pink striped wool cloak which reached to his knees. His loose, muddy, brown pants were tattered and frayed, and on his big feet he wore cork-like sandals. Under a red cap, straight black hair hung in a long braid draped over his shoulder.

"Hello? I'm sorry, but what did you say?" Manuela absently shook out her skirt and put some stray curls behind her ears. The man stood there with his silly grin and stared at her. "Hello? Look, can you help get my sister out of this hole?" She pointed at the opening where Fritz was sitting.

"Kawkis Unstanta?" the little man asked. Clearly, he had no idea what Manuela wanted. This was going to be difficult.

"Sister. In hole. Get out." Manuela pantomimed the situation exaggerating the motions over and over. The little man just stood there and kept grinning. Getting frustrated, Manuela picked up the cord, which was still wrapped around Fritz. "I'm trying to get someone out of there. Don't you understand? What are you smiling at?" She threw the cord down and sat down with her arms crossed.

The dark-skinned man cocked his head but kept smiling. "Janiw yakti," he replied.

"Great. I suppose that means, 'I'm laughing at your silly dance and circus outfit.'" Manuela walked over to the hole ignoring the man.

"No. I always smiling. Do not know why. Come this way. We get sister. Then we eat. I help. You see." The little man walked past her and scrambled over the ridge. At the top he looked back grinning. "You come?"

Manuela couldn't believe it. "Why didn't you just say you could speak English in the first place," she said angrily. "Alright. Let me grab my backpack," Manuela said. She grabbed her pack and, after untying Fritz, stashed the cord in her pack. She wasn't getting anywhere by herself here anyway, and the little man seemed so confident. Climbing the ridge she raced after the swift stranger and followed him to another ridge with big rocks along it. Without effort, he pushed aside one of the rocks and exposed a crawlspace that went deep into the mountain. Putting his finger to his lips he motioned for her to be silent and then disappeared inside. Fritz followed the little man, wagging his tail. Manuela hesitated only a moment; then she crouched down and entered into the darkness.

Chapter 5

The girls find a friend

WHEN HER SCREAM ENDED Silvia snapped her mouth shut and took shallow breaths. The rat looked a little disoriented with the light shining in its eyes. At least as big as a Chihuahua, the black rat seemed to be sneering at her. Its big red eyes didn't seem to have pupils, and Silvia thought it looked like it was licking its chops. Altogether it was definitely scarier than anything she had ever seen. The longer she waited for the rat to pounce, the more afraid she became. But he wouldn't move. He just sat there sneering and slathering.

As she stood there frozen, she noticed a small stone glinting near the rat's feet. Gasping, Silvia forgot for the moment of how scared she was. Holding the flashlight steady with her left hand, she reached down to pat the pocket in her skirt. The *shaanti! It must have fallen out when I slipped down the hole*, she thought. At least she hadn't lost it in the tunnel. But how was she going to get it now? If she moved, she was sure the rat would pounce on her. Maybe she could scare the rat away? But how? Silvia's mind raced with possibilities. *At least now I'm thinking*, she thought wryly.

Summoning up all her courage, Silvia squinted up her face, stuck out her tongue and began waving the flashlight at the rat, all the while yelling "Ahgagagagaga Ahgagagagaga!" as loud as she could.

The rat didn't move.

"Get out of here, you ugly thing!" she shouted, kicking stones toward the rat.

"Whoya callin' ugly, Moonface!" said the rat, in a gravelly squeak. Silvia jumped back, hitting her pack against the rock.

"Was that you?" Silvia asked. Her hands were trembling and the light was flickering around the rat like some crazy laser show.

"No. It was da rock. Dumb. How yous got dis far, I dunno." The rat waddled over to the *shaanti* and sat down in front of it.

"Rats don't talk. Are you a rat?" Silvia kept looking from the *shaanti* to the rat's bulging red eyes.

"I *look* like a rat, right? Well, I bite like one too," the rat gave a feral grin, saliva dripping down onto his scaly claws.

Silvia was disgusted. If she weren't so in shock, she might have thrown up. However, the guilt about the lost *shaanti* was just as powerful as her disbelief and fear. A talking rat? This couldn't be a coincidence. This had to be one of Shatru's Rogs that Miss Sasha had told them about. But a rat? Silvia had imagined big ape-like monsters, not a little slobbering rat. But his teeth were glinting in the flashlight's feeble ray, and Silvia wasn't going to argue with him about biting.

"You girls is fools," he said with his pinched up voice. "Yous never make it to castle. Dis *shaanti* here, is mine. Yous can't even last one day!" The rat let out what Silvia thought was meant to be a laugh. "I can get a good price from dee Rogs for it." The rat leaned over and licked the blue, glittery stone.

Silvia fought off a gag. "You mean you're not a Rog?" she asked.

"Me? A Rog? Sheesh, dumb is too smart for yous. See ya." The rat picked up the *shaanti* between his teeth and quickly scurried around into the darkness.

"Wait! You can't take that! We need it to get out of here!" Silvia waved the flashlight around frantically trying to keep track of the rat. She saw him scurry to one of the other large holes that she had checked earlier. He jumped in, but as soon as she got to the other side of the cavern, he came tumbling out in a violet flash, the *shaanti* flying out of his mouth and landing near Silvia. Fighting the urge to vomit, she grabbed the stone and thrust it deep into her skirt pocket, keeping her light steady on the fallen rat. He scrambled back onto his legs and ran screeching across the cavern and into the hole that Silvia was so excited about before he appeared.

All Manuela could smell was feet. At least that was what it seemed like. Thousands of stinky feet. In the complete darkness, holding onto Fritz, Manuela imagined the tunnel not made out of rock, but millions of tiny toes wiggling with toe jam. She kept her nose plugged with her other hand as she squeezed down the low tunnel.

"Are we almost to her?" she asked, not letting go of her nose.

41

"It the smell, yes? I used to it, now. These mushrooms. Not good eat, but good for heal many things. Not good smell, O.K." The little man's deep voice flowed back to her. In the dark his voice made him sound tall and regal. "Quiet now. I need do something. You and dog don't move when I stop. Remember." Manuela walked a few paces and then felt Fritz stop. Bumping into the dog slightly, she stepped back and waited. What was he going to do in this hole? Manuela wondered at the coincidence of him finding her right at this moment. What if he were one of the Rogs Miss Sasha warned them about? Manuela held onto Fritz's collar tightly and waited.

"Now I do something you don't see before. Stay, remember." The deep voice seemed very quiet in front of her, barely a whisper. Suddenly she heard stones moving ahead of her and then the tunnel lit up with a blinding violet light and she closed her eyes tightly trying not to be afraid. She heard a low chuckle from the little man.

"Is over. Sister will be O.K." Manuela felt the small hand pat her hand that was still tightly holding on to Fritz. "We go in there now and you tell her follow us out. We don't stay. O.K.?" The little man had a small light coming from behind his other hand and Manuela's eyes adjusted to the little glow. His smooth face seemed sinister in the shadow, but Manuela had no choice. If Silvia was 'in there,' then the most important thing was to be together.

He turned around and ducked into the narrowing passage. Fritz and Manuela followed until she found herself stepping out into an underground cavern. Silvia stood against one wall shining her flashlight on them like she was a member of a S.W.A.T. team. When Silvia saw Manuela, her tense face softened and she ran to her sister giving her a big hug.

"Oh, Manu, it's you. I thought the Rogs, because the rat ... and the light ... Oh, Manu!" Silvia buried her face into her sister's shoulder.

Manuela was just as excited to see Silvia. "What rat? Oh, Silvi, how did you get here? Let's just get out of here, O.K.?" Manuela said.

Silvia let go of Manuela to hug Fritz and looked over warily at the smooth-faced little man. He had his goofy grin on again, and Manuela remembered what he had said. "Silvia, we had better just follow him out and then we can figure things out." Manuela picked up Silvia's beat up hat and pulled it over Silvia's dirty curls. Then she nodded at the stranger and followed as he turned back into the tunnel.

Once they emerged back into the sunlight, the stranger kept walking down towards the lake. In silence, holding hands, Manuela led Silvia behind him. Silvia seemed shaken by what had happened and was not speaking. She kept squeezing her sister's hand. Around them, Fritz bounded in zigzags, happy to be out of the tunnel.

Since Silvia didn't seem to mind, Manuela just kept following the little man. Remembering what he had said about food, she thought it best just to trust him for now. Maybe he could even help them get to Kalahuta. The day was warming up even more with warm breezes getting more frequent as they approached the shore. The rotten smell also got stronger. At the shore, the small man turned and wrinkled his nose. "Is bad smell here, too. Not always so. Lake full of bad things. Many bad things come down river from city." He pointed to the far left.

Silvia seemed to come out of her trance when he spoke. Manuela smiled, knowing her sister could not stay down for long. Taking off her hat and pushing her hair back behind her ears, Silvia gave the stranger a smile. "Thank you, sir. You saved much more than my life back there," she said adjusting her hat back on her head.

Manuela looked at her confused. "What happened down there, Silvi?" she asked.

"She tell us after eat. I take to my house. We eat. Then we talk of many things." Turning, the little man started walking down the beach to what Manuela saw was a little boat.

"Eat!" Silvia practically yelled. She gave Manuela a big grin and trotted after Fritz.

Once everyone was on the boat, the stranger pushed the little craft into the water with a pole. It was about 12 feet long with pointed ends, like a canoe. But instead of being carved out of one piece of wood, this boat was like a big basket, woven together with thousands of what Manuela thought were reeds. A little apprehensive about the strength of a basket boat, Manuela sat up straight and gripped the shoulder straps on her pack.

"Not to worry," the little man laughed, his deep guffaw at odds with his goofy smile. "Totora boat very strong. Even old islands made from reed. Very old skill." He reached into his gaudy cloak and pulled out a dirty muslin cloth and started to unwrap it. Manuela wasn't so sure about whole islands made out of reeds, but she relaxed a little when she saw how comfortable Fritz seemed. In fact, Fritz seemed to take to the stranger very well, even curling up around his big feet in the boat. Silvia had been silent, but now that her rescuer had spoken, she looked up at him curiously. From inside the cloth he pulled out chunks of brown bread and a lump of dark yellow something which he began to rip apart. Fritz got up and wagged his tail and sniffed the man's lap.

"Fritz, don't bother … um … the man," Silvia didn't know how to address him.

"Is O.K. Some for all. My name Aruwiri. You call me Aru." Aru put a piece of the yellow lump and a piece of bread on the floor of the boat for Fritz. Then he handed Silvia and Manuela the same. "For now, yes. Then at home, I make big meal and we talk."

"Thank you," Manuela said. She picked up her bread. Sniffing it she decided that her hunger overrode the apparently stale hunk. Silvia was already chewing hers.

"Aru," Silvia said, already comfortable with this new turn of events, "What is this yellow stuff? Some kind of old potato?"

"Is chuno. I make it in spring. Like old potato, yes." Fritz had already finished and was settling down again against Aru's feet. Manuela watched Silvia try the chuno. She made a face but continued to eat. *Well*, Manuela thought, *Silvi may be able to eat anything when she is hungry, but I think I'll just save mine for a real emergency.* Waiting for Aru to turn away with his pole, Manuela slipped the chuno into her skirt pocket. Her fingers touched the compass and she pulled it out.

"Silvia, I found your compass by the shore. You really should be more careful," Manuela said, holding out the compass.

Silvia scrunched up her face and grabbed the compass. She looked overly agitated and she reached into her own pocket.

"You still have the *shaanti* in there?" Manuela whispered. "Why don't you give it to me since I will use it next. I will put it in my pack where it will be safe."

"And if you loose your pack?" Silvia scowled. "Don't worry, it's in here. I'll give it to you later," she said quietly. Her eyes looked over at Aru, who was looking off towards the mountains. He was chewing some leaves that made his teeth an unappetizing green. Manuela sighed. It probably wasn't a good idea to reveal too much to Aru yet. But they did owe him for getting Silvia out. Manuela couldn't wait to hear what really happened down there.

Finally, they saw land ahead. It seemed to be one of the islands. *Maybe he can help us even more,* thought Manuela. *Maybe he can help us find Kalahuta, at least.* Aru stood up slowly and maneuvered the boat with his pole until they were close. Jumping out, he held the craft steady and grinned at the girls, while Fritz jumped in and paddled up the shore. "Welcome, my home. Kalahuta."

Chapter 6

Meeting the DragonFlies

INSIDE ARU'S REED HUT the light was dim and comforting. He had hung woven shawls over the windows and it left the place cooler. The furnishings were simple: a low mattress against the far wall with a blue covering, a few reed mats lying around, and many colorfully woven cloths hung around the wall. Bamboo poles lined the walls, keeping the reeds in place. Near the back of the hut was a hole with cooking utensils around it, and a low wood table behind it held a few black pots and various sized baskets made out of the inevitable totora reed. The girls had learned from Aru that the reed was the mainstay of the area, being used for everything from mats and shoes to boats, huts and actual ancient floating islands. The baskets held more chuno and also tunta, roots that the natives of the area processed by smashing and baking in the heat of the sun or, in the case of tunta, immersing in water for weeks before they were left in the sun to bake.

Aru had surprised them when he had said his home was Kalahuta. Silvia had seen Manuela's mouth drop a little when he grabbed her pack and hoisted her into the cool water. Silvia had hopped over to avoid the same fate, and the girls had exchanged meaningful glances. When Aru had finally deposited them inside his hut and gave them each fresh water from a bucket that sat next to his cooking hole, Silvia couldn't help but remember Miss Sasha's words; *I have the words to take you to Kalahuta. After that you must find the Weaver. He is your contact.* Was Aru a Weaver? Besides the totora boat, the hut's walls were adorned with every conceivable scene woven in beautiful rainbow colors. When Aru had left to gather things for the meal, Silvia turned to Manuela excitedly.

"He's the Weaver, isn't he, Manu? He's got to be our contact," she said.

"We don't know that yet, Silvia. Now give me the *shaanti* and tell me what happened." Manuela held out her palm but gave Silvia a reassuring smile.

Silvia sighed and reached in her skirt pocket. Slowly she opened her palm to look at the stone. It was muddy from its adventures underground. She passed it to Manuela who gave it a long look. Silvia told her what happened.

"If it weren't for me, Fritz, and Aru, you would have not only lost yourself but the *shaanti* as well," said Manuela angrily.

"Thanks a lot, Manu. Don't you even care that a talking rat almost ate me? And he knew about Rogs." But Silvia didn't protest too much. She knew Manuela was right about her carelessness, and she didn't want to dwell on it. "The fact that Aru scared that thing away is sure proof that he must be our contact. How else could he have …" Silvia broke off as she saw Fritz pad over to the door. Aru lifted the blue woven blanket that covered the doorway and brought in a big burlap sack which he carried over to the cooking hole.

"You see. Soon I have stew ready and then you feel better," Aru said. Lighting a little fire, he placed a pot over the flame and then sprinkled in some mixture from a pouch he brought out of his pocket. The spicy smell wafted over to the girls, and Silvia thought the smell was familiar. Suddenly, she knew it.

"Is that … samudra, Aru?" Silvia asked. She heard Manuela take a sharp breath. The appley smell was distinct, and if he didn't know what they were talking about, then they hadn't really revealed anything. If it were samudra, however, then they could almost be sure he was the Weaver.

"Why, yes. Ah, you do not know yet. Yes. I am Weaver. I have been waiting for Miss Sasha to send you for long, long time." Aru's deep voice seemed to fill the hut. He walked over and sat on a mat next to the girls.

"But how could you know who we were?" Manuela said.

"How could I not? Two young girls who not know speak my tongue. Two who come from nowhere to the lake and are hunted." Silvia tensed and grabbed at her skirt. "Yes, little one. Tell me what happened with rat in old silver mine. I know rat. He is here to watch me. He knows about the magic, but is not good." Aru got up to finish his cooking.

While Aru cooked, Silvia retold her story with the rat, and then the girls added the rest of their story so far. Aru listened silently, not interrupting. Finally, he placed a steaming bowl of stew in front of each of them, including Fritz. Silvia looked at the hot food with excitement. While the chuno was sort of like chewing on shoelaces, it had stopped her grumbling stomach. This, however, would fill that gnawing hole. The warm cinnamon apple scent filled the air and she took the warm bread Aru brought from the cooking hole and dipped it in. Aru told them it was a mixture of barley, quinoa, fish and potatoes with a little wild celery and, of course, samudra.

After Fritz and the girls hungrily devoured the stew, Aru put the bowls in a bucket and brought a basket over from the shelf. He passed it to Silvia who peered inside.

"What's this, Aru? Are they cookies? Because I love cookies," Silvia said with a smile.

"Yes. These are special. I make them of quinoa and samudra. Very strong. Very ... important for your journey." Aru nodded at Silvia. "Take one now. Then, please, put rest in packs. They are my gift for journey. They make you strong in magic and truth," said Aru.

Silvia understood. She picked out one of the square brown crisps and handed the basket to Manuela who did the same. Then Aru took the basket and tossed one to Fritz who wagged his tail happily. Silvia and Manuela both bit into the crisps at the same time. Instantly, Silvia's melted in her mouth sending an intense heat rush through her, which made her open her eyes wide. She noticed Manuela reacting similarly. After finishing the cookie with a few more bites, Silvia noticed the room was swirling with a blue color. Blue lines were blurring all around them, but when she put her hand out it passed right through the color as if it were smoke. Aru was grinning goofily and chuckling. "Look closely, little one. Maybe they will stop and say hello," he said.

Cocking her head, Silvia tried to focus on the swirling lines. Finally, she saw them; tiny little flies were buzzing about the room! But why hadn't she seen them before? Looking even closer, Silvia saw that the flies looked like little people with wings, like fairies in books.

"Magic DragonFlies," Manuela said with wonder. She was sitting still with her hands in her lap. Silvia stared harder still. Whirling by in quick patterns, the DragonFlies seemed barely to notice them. Once, one stopped right in front of Silvia and cocked its head like hers. Silvia smiled and so did the DragonFly. He was gold and had double wings like a dragonfly that were a translucent blue. Around him flowed a blue mist covering most of his body and streaming down his back like flowing hair. The DragonFly bowed his head and then looked up quickly winking and flitting off.

"Manu, that one just said hello, I think," Silvia said softly. Suddenly the blue lines whirled more quickly and then they zoomed off through a crack in the door flap. Fritz came out from the corner where he was hiding and snuggled between the two girls. No one moved for a few minutes while they thought about what just happened. Finally, Silvia reached for her pack and, taking out her orange velvet bag, began filling it with half of the crisps remaining in the basket. Manuela wordlessly did the same, filling up her blue velvet bag. Neither of them spoke, but each knew that these crisps would probably be very important later on, and they didn't intend on eating them like candy. Aru said nothing as he watched them, only grinning goofily until they had re-buckled their packs.

"DragonFlies only come when you reach out with soul and call. But samudra always good. Now time to sleep. Before dawn we wake and we go to special place. There I show you words for *shaanti*. They will take you to new place. There you will meet next contact. I only know this. DragonFly Keeper is in much danger. The magic is dying. Not as many DragonFlies. I know words to take you to a contact that know more. You need *shaanti*. You have *shaanti*, yes?" Aru looked calmly at the girls.

"I have it now. We will keep it safe, Aru," Manuela said, giving Silvia a sideways glance. Silvia rolled her eyes. Why did Manuela have to make a big deal out of every mistake she made? She didn't mean to do things without thinking. It just always seemed that the thing to do was the first thing she thought of. *Well, Miss Manuela,* she thought, *I'll make sure you remember when* you *make a mistake.*

Manuela didn't know why she opened her eyes until she felt Aru gently tapping her shoulder. In the dark hut, she could just make out Silvia sleeping next to her, curled up on another woven mat. Silvia's hair was sticking out all over the place and her hands were curled up tightly under her chin. Fritz was snuggled under the blanket that Silvia was rolled up in, but he was awake and watching as Manuela sat up and started packing her blanket away and then put her hat on. When she was ready, Manuela pulled the blanket off of Silvia and packed it in Silvia's pack; of course, Silvia slept on peacefully like she always did. *How does she do that?* thought Manuela. *I couldn't sleep well at all in this weird place.* Finally, she knocked hard on her sister's legs while Fritz gave Silvia sloppy kisses on her face.

"O.K., O.K., I'm awake ..." Silvia said, as she turned over and buried her face in her arms.

"Come on, Silvi. Aru says it's time to go. The moon is full and we need to get going," Manuela said. Silvia finally opened her eyes and sat up. Manuela stuck her hat on her head and pulled her up, handing Silvia her pack. Aru put a finger to his lips for silence and then lead the group out of the hut.

Outside the sky was full of stars despite the full moon. The air was extremely chilly and Manuela was glad that they had gone to bed wearing their sweaters. Aru had not told them where they were headed, but Manuela hoped it wasn't anywhere really cold. Marching silently down towards the shore, Manuela could hear the night sounds of insects, which stopped while they passed and began again as they continued on down the path. An owl, or some kind of night bird, flew by in front of them, startling Fritz. Manuela was surprised that she wasn't more frightened. Usually Silvia was the brave one, and Manuela stayed back a little assessing the situation. Sometimes it bothered her that Silvia didn't see her hesitation as cautiousness; instead she seemed to act as if Manuela were afraid of everything. Behind her Silvia trudged along silently, still half dozing while walking. *I hope she learned her lesson falling in that hole,* she thought. *I can't spend the entire trip looking after her. We will never save the DragonFly Keeper that way.* Manuela shifted her pack and got ready to get on Aru's totora raft.

The water was calm, not like the night before, and the girls sat calmly listening to the quiet lap of the water against the boat.

"Are you sure you don't know where we are going, Aru?" Silvia asked.

"No, little one. I know only words to get you there. They are strange to me. Another language. I know only their sounds." Aru stared out at the mountains as he maneuvered the raft towards another island. "I do know that it is much danger there. More than little rat. Remember to call the DragonFlies if you need them." Finally they reached the shore and the girls jumped out holding their boots and socks to keep them dry. Manuela's breath caught as she hit the chilly water. Behind her, she could see that the cold water had the same affect on Silvia as an alarm clock. Back on shore the girls tied on their boots and followed Aru up a hill. Looking back at the lake, Manuela couldn't help but note how beautifully it sparkled in the moonlight. It glowed. The dark mountains seemed to encircle it like fingers cupping the diamond waters. Turning, she followed Aru down another path.

"This Island of the Sun. We come here to climb the stairs of Yumani," said Aru without turning around. The girls sidestepped many puddles that seemed almost permanent features of the path. Cold air prickled Manuela's cheeks, and she started to get used to the rotten tomato smell. Silvia seemed more alert now and Manuela giggled when she heard Silvia's stomach growling.

"I sure am hungry. Aren't you, Manu?" Silvia asked rubbing her hands together.

"Not hungry enough to eat this chuno that is still in my pocket," Manuela said. "Here, do you want it? I think I'll wait and take my chances." Manuela handed the leathery strip to Silvia who wrinkled her nose but then bit into it.

Finally, Aru led the girls to a higher hill along a path with a low loose stone wall running next to it. At the top of the hill he set down the burlap sack he was carrying and motioned for the girls to sit. Fritz snuggled up against Aru's feet. When they were all sitting in a circle, Aru opened his sack and brought out some strange fruits.

"We need good breakfast. Here this *granadilla*." Aru handed one of the little fruits to each of the girls. He also passed them little knives. Hungry, they ripped opened the flesh and let the goopy fruit flop into their mouth in one big glop. It tasted a little like passion fruit.

"Here, this *lu'cuma*. And this my favorite," Aru said handing them small, striped, orange and green fruit the size of peaches. "I eat every morning." Manuela and Silvia cut into the curious fruits and took bites. It was cool and fresh and tasted like melon. Not a lover of fruit, Fritz was content chewing on the chuno that Silvia had discarded.

Revitalized from the pre-dawn picnic, the girls rubbed their cold hands together and waited for the next step. Manuela watched their breath cloud out in front of them and really hoped that it would be warmer where they were going. Reaching into the bottom of his sack, Aru pulled out two little packages wrapped in muslin cloth. He handed one to each of the girls.

"These are gifts. Friend to friend. Is important to remember friend this way," said Aru. He nodded then, and Silvia and Manuela carefully unwrapped the presents. Inside Manuela's was a very small wafer with the heady cinnamon apple smell of samudra and a tiny circle woven from wool. The circle had tiny gray and white feathers attached around the rim which were soft and downy. Silvia had the same.

"Eat samudra disk now for warmth. The sun tokens are for you to remember your strengths. Do not think of what you cannot do. Think of what you can do. This is important for journey." Aru winked and popped a wafer in his grinning mouth. Manuela and Silvia, now accustomed to the samudra effect, quickly ate theirs, letting the disks melt on their tongues. Instantly Manuela felt warmer and stronger.

After carefully re-wrapping her miniature 'sun', Manuela put it deep inside her pack. *But what can I give Aru? We would never have found him on our own,* Manuela thought, digging around her pack. Finally, she pulled out the little flute that Miss Sasha had packed for her.

"Aru," she said thrusting out the flute, "this is for you. I don't know if you can use it, but I would like to give you something as well." Aru smiled and took the flute, bringing it to his lips. Suddenly the quiet night filled with insect sounds was vibrating with a beautiful hollow note. Aru continued to play for a few minutes creating a sad melody that echoed in her ears when he put the flute inside his coat.

"Ah, young traveler, you have given me a gift worth more than you know. For those who can play its special tunes, this flute is magical. Thank you." Aru placed his hand on her folded knee and bowed his head. Manuela heard Silvia rummaging in her pack. Not to be outdone, she quickly produced the little red bowl Miss Sasha had packed for her.

"I know that you already have many bowls and baskets, Aru, but this is all I have. And I want to give you something," Silvia sighed. Aru lifted his hand and, smiling, accepted Silvia's little red bowl. Winking at her he put his hand over the top and then closed his eyes. After murmuring a few things that the girls couldn't quite make out, he opened his eyes wide and smiled his goofy grin, lifting his palm from the bowl. Leaning over, Silvia and Manuela looked inside. It was filled with samudra wafers!

"How did you do that? I thought that was just a little clay bowl?" Silvia asked, staring at the pile of samudra.

"Ah, little one. You have made me a rich, rich man. I am very grateful for your gift." He wrapped up the bowl and wafers in a cloth he produced from under his coat and then placed a hand on each of the girls' knees. "Now is time to say goodbye. I cannot go. Only you. But take my gifts and I am with you." He bowed his head and then stood up. Manuela and Silvia got up and adjusted their dusty skirts. Silvia took off her beat-up hat and handed it to Aru.

"You can have this too, Aru. I really don't want it anymore." Aru laughed and put it on top of his red cap on his head. Silvia scratched her curls vigorously, causing them to spring out in every direction. Manuela couldn't help laughing. They certainly looked like two crazies right now. Manuela took off her hat and shook out her curls too. Fritz gave a bark and did a doggy shake to join in. Finally, they stopped jiggling around when they saw Aru raise his hands.

"Now is the time. The *shaanti*," he said solemnly.

Manuela pulled out the glittering blue stone. In the moonlight it looked alive and fiery. Folding in her right hand, she grabbed Silvia's hand and held on tightly. Silvia took a hold of Fritz's red collar and they waited.

"Listen first. You must get words right first time. I repeat them over and over until you ready. Then you nod. I am silent and you will go. Now. Close eyes and listen." Aru gave them one last goofy grin. Manuela closed her eyes tightly and inhaled. The night air was crisp and invigorating. Silvia gripped her left hand. Finally, Aru began to speak the special words that would take them to a new place, a new adventure, and closer to saving the Dragonfly Keeper.

"*Sapnis. Spane,*" Aru paused. "*Sapnis. Spane,*" he said again. He continued to speak these two words over and over. *That's it?* Manuela thought. *Sapnis Spane. Sapnis Spane. I wonder what it means and what language that is.* Fearful of what was going to happen next, Manuela kept repeating the words to herself until she felt an unmistakably extra strong tug on her left arm. Manuela nodded, and Aru stopped. Clearing her throat, Manuela took one last deep breath and said, *"Sapnis. Spane."*

Chapter 7

The girls find out about boars

THIS TIME SILVIA WAS PREPARED for the sudden temperature change and the dizzy feeling. This time, however, she didn't know in advance where they would end up. The cool air whipped around and then settled into a warmer moist feeling. She felt her balance falter and she tumbled backwards onto what felt like smooth cool grass. Opening her eyes slowly, she was surprised to see the sun was already in the sky. Manuela was rubbing her eyes, trying to adjust to the light change. All around them were big trees and rolling hills. For a moment, Silvia thought they were back in Ohio.

"Well, goodbye, Bolivia, I guess," Manuela said as she squinted around. Silvia just sat up and peeled off her sweater.

"I wish we had a change of clothes. I mean, these things are dirty and smelly and uncomfortable and ..."

"Silvi, stop complaining. Do you think for once you could focus on the real problem instead of yourself?" Manuela took off her sweater and neatly folded it into her pack. Silvia just rolled her eyes and got up. They were in the clearing of a forest; that was clear. Big spruce trees and pines towered all around them, closing them in on all four sides. The air was sweet, and Silvia heard the gurgling of water nearby.

"Well, I'm not just thinking of myself. You look pretty awful yourself, you know," Silvia said with a huff. Pulling her canteen out of her pack, she walked towards a big fallen trunk and sat down on it. Manuela sighed and joined her on the log with her own canteen.

"Look, Silvi. I'm sorry. It's just that we have been looking for the DragonFly Keeper for over a day, and we know no more than when we were at Miss Sasha's. We *have* to find a way to get better information." Manuela picked a little at the bark of the fallen log and threw it into the soft grass as she took a long drink from the Bolivian water from Aru.

"Even when we find the Keeper, how will we free him? I can only imagine what Shatru is like," Silvia said. "I wish I would have had a chance to get that disgusting rat to talk more." She slapped at a fly that was crawling at her arm.

"Silvia, we can't just wait for you to fall in a hole this time to find the next contact," Manuela smiled. "*Please* don't fall into a hole this time."

Silvia smiled back and then bit her lip slightly. "Hey. I think I remember the rat saying something about us not ever being able to get to the castle. Do you think that is where Shatru is keeping the DragonFly Keeper? Or maybe we will find out more at a castle." Silvia took a long drink.

"Well, I guess that's all we have to go on. We don't even know where we are now, let alone where we are going. Let's see if we can find some water; I'm getting really thirsty, and we should fill up these canteens while we can," Manuela said, getting up and stretching. Fritz sniffed at the bark they had thrown. Deciding it wasn't food, he circled happily when the girls started walking towards the gurgling sound, deep within the trees.

As they approached the edge of the clearing, Silvia spotted bushes filled with berries. Calling for Manuela, she raced ahead and started picking handfuls. When she started to pop one in her mouth, she heard Manuela call out and stopped.

"Silvia! You don't know what those are! Maybe they are poisonous berries," Manuela said breathlessly. She was leaning over with her hands on her knees, spent from running after Silvia. "Do you even know what they are?"

"Manu! These are cranberries!" Silvia shouted. "I am going to eat a million!" She began to shove the tart berries in her mouth. Manuela picked one and looked at it. But Silvia didn't care if Manuela believed her or not. She wasn't as picky, and she definitely was hungry. It would take a lot of cranberries to fill her up.

After she had her fill, Silvia laid back in the grass by the bushes and sighed. She usually ate a lot, even though her thin frame didn't show it. Aru's fruit was good, but it definitely didn't fill her up for long. She gazed up into the trees and the sky, watching birds jump from branch to branch when she heard something that definitely wasn't a bird. Turning her head, Silvia sat up slowly and tried to see what had just made the loud snort. Manuela was a few yards away picking berries with Fritz. Suddenly Fritz wheeled around and started barking in the direction Silvia was looking. The bushes rustled and Silvia jumped up scrambling backwards towards Manuela.

Snorting loudly, a big hairy black pig was charging straight at her. She fell and rolled sideways just in time. The pig squealed and then stopped, turning towards Manuela and Fritz. "Run, Manu! That thing has huge pointy tusks!" Silvia yelled.

The pig turned, clearly undecided on whom to attack first. The moment's hesitation was enough for Fritz. He ran a few steps closer to the giant pig, barking and growling. Immediately the huge, hairy animal clawed the ground and ran full steam towards Fritz. Fritz gingerly jumped sideways and ran into the bushes barking and growling. Silvia was huddled under a bush watching, as was Manuela, and they watched as the boar turned and ran after Fritz into the forest.

Neither girl made a sound at first, but then Silvia crawled out from the bush and trotted towards Manuela crying.

"Silvia! Are you O.K.? What happened to your face?" Manuela grabbed her sister when she saw her and tried to wipe the red on her cheeks. "Oh, Silvi, it's only cranberry juice!" Manuela hugged her sister close. Silvia was shaking silently now and she buried her face in her sister's shoulder.

"But what about Fritz?" Silvia whimpered. "We have to go after him. He saved our lives." Wiping her eyes, Silvia regained her composure and looked around for her pack. Grabbing it she started off in the direction Fritz had run.

"Wait, Silvia! Wait for me!" Manuela yelled trying to keep up with her. Silvia could see the big pig's muddy prints at first, but then when the ground shifted uphill, they seemed to disappear into the pine needles that covered the ground. Deeper in the forest, there were fewer bushes and grasses, and Silvia slowed down when she realized she had no idea which direction they could have gone. Finally, Manuela caught up with her and grabbed her arm.

"Listen," Manuela said quietly. Silvia listened. She didn't hear anything but the twitter of squirrels and the cry of a few birds.

"What?"

"Shhh. Listen longer." Manuela put her finger to her lips. Silvia waited. Then she heard it. It was Fritz barking! She turned and looked at Manuela who pointed to their right. Walking briskly, the girls made their way toward the top of a hill and looked down. About fifty yards away was a swiftly moving river. They heard the bark again and hurried down to the bank of the river towards it. The babbling of the river made it difficult for them to pinpoint where Fritz was, but then he barked again and they saw him lying behind a bush near the water.

Silvia ran over and bent down to see his right back flank torn and bleeding. He licked her face weakly when she bent down to hug him. "Oh, Fritz, what happened? Manuela, we need to find him help."

"We need to stop the bleeding in his leg first, Silvia." Manuela ripped a long piece from the bottom of her skirt. After rinsing it in the river, she poured water on Fritz's leg with the canteen and began wrapping it around the wound. Silvia ripped two long strips off of her skirt, leaving it a mini. She rinsed them and gave them to Manuela and then got out her orange velvet bag. Carefully, she took out a samudra crisp and brought it over to Fritz. Eagerly, Fritz ate up the crisp and drank the water the girls offered him, finally laying down his head and closing his eyes to rest.

After they were sure Fritz was comfortable, the girls took off their clunky boots and waded in the river. Silvia wanted to rinse out their socks and sweaters, but Manuela had pointed out that it was no fun to walk in wet socks. Silvia grumbled. Why did she have to do what Manuela said anyway? But, of course, Manuela had made sense. They didn't know how long they had before they needed those socks again. After rinsing their faces, they climbed out of the water and Silvia stayed next to Fritz while Manuela propped her pack behind her and sat under a nearby birch tree.

"Don't worry Fritz, we will find the contact, and I'm sure he will be able to help." Silvia said soothingly as she tried to think of what they could do next. "Maybe we should split up, Manu. You could stay here with Fritz, and I could go looking for someone. I'm sure Aru's words must have brought us close to the contact." Silvia stroked Fritz's matted golden fur. His breathing was relaxed and the bleeding had stopped. They wouldn't know until later if he had any broken bones.

"No way, Silvia. That's how we got into trouble last time," Manuela said.

"Well, we can't just leave him here, all alone. What do you propose we do, then?" Silvia said flippantly.

"That's exactly what I propose we do," Manuela said crossing over to Silvia and Fritz. "He needs to rest, and there isn't anything more we can do for him now anyway. If we follow the river," Manuela looked downstream, "then we will be able to come back for him easily."

"But that big pig might come back!" Silvia said frowning. "Or what if a Rog gets him?"

"Come on, Silvi," Manuela said crouching down next to them. "You know it's what we have to do. We need to find someone to help him, and we need to figure out how to get more information on the Keeper." She stroked Fritz gently. "He will be fine for a few hours. I'm sure if there are people around here that they will be close to the water. Let's go before we waste any more time." Getting up, Manuela grabbed her pack and started off downstream. Silvia waited, but when she saw that Manuela wasn't even going to look back, she quickly grabbed her pack and bent down to kiss Fritz.

"Don't worry boy," she said quietly. "I won't be gone for long."

"It's raining," said Silvia.

"No, it's just misty."

"No, it's raining, and my socks are wet anyway. But they smell because they aren't clean," Silvia said. Manuela could hear her clomping behind like an elephant.

"So don't smell. And don't talk either, please," Manuela said. They had been walking for a long time and she was getting frustrated herself. Silvia, however, had very little patience to begin with. Manuela's stomach was grumbling, too, and she *knew* how Silvia got when *she* was hungry. Still, Silvia could try and not be so whiny.

"I'm hungry, but all I smell is socks." Silvia stopped walking and crashed down onto the ground with a loud thump. Manuela turned around and looked down at her.

"Did you save any berries? Because I have a few in my pocket." Manuela pulled out the warm mushy berries.

"No thank you, Miss think-of-everything. Even if I *could* bring myself to eat more cranberries, I think that goopy mess you have there would ruin them for the rest of my life," Silvia said, flopping back with her arms wide. "I want bread. Pizza. I want pizza with pepperoni, onions, and mushrooms," she said dreamily with her eyes closed.

"Sorry, miss. We only have warm cranberry mush, or tree bark," Manuela said laughing. She threw her pack down by an old oak tree and sat down. The misty air smelled good, apart from their dirty-dog smell. It was nutty, almost spicy. She took a deep breath and sat back against the tree. The sun was hiding behind clouds, and the air was a little cool. *Where could we be? There has to be a reason why we are meant to be here,* thought Manuela.

"Do you remember hiking by Aunt Tina's in Vermont?" asked Silvia. "Doesn't this forest remind you of the trails there?"

"Sort of. But that forest had so many thorns and grasses growing in it. This forest is just ... well, just trees and moss." Manuela looked around her. It was true that she had thought of the forests in New England too. But she knew they couldn't be there. For one thing, things felt older.

"Hey, Manu," Silvia asked quietly, "what is that huge bird?" Turning slowly to see farther downstream, Manuela looked to where Silvia was pointing. There, wading in the river was a huge white bird with a big long beak. Its long legs looked like they couldn't possibly hold it up. It turned towards them and then put its face back in the water, coming back up with a wriggling fish. Gulping it down, the bird slowly stalked back up the bank, turned around and took off over the river, beating its huge wings to raise it high over the trees.

"Wow, that was a big bird, Silvi," Manuela said staring after it.

"You mean, that was a big fish. I'm starving. Come on. We *have* to find someone before I start eating leaves." Silvia shouldered her pack and moved downstream. Manuela got up quickly and headed after her. She was sure they would have found people by now. The *shaanti* and its words should have brought them very close to their contact.

By now the sun was high in the sky, and the misty rain had cleared. Manuela tried smoothing her hair back into the rubber band, but it just sprang out in frizzy curls around her face. Up ahead, Silvia looked like she had snakes wiggling out from her head. Manuela was afraid she must look the same. She was starting to get genuinely discouraged when she saw a little hut a little farther ahead. Silvia must have seen it too because she picked up her pace.

The girls approached without saying a word. The hut was really small and quaint with a small garden in the back. Leading from the riverbank to the front door was a well-used stone path bordered with little pretty flowers of all colors. Silvia reached the hut first and miraculously waited for Manuela.

"This doesn't look like your castle, Silvi," Manuela said. But neither girl was disappointed. The little wooden hut was neatly painted white and there was a wonderful baking smell coming out of the open window. Slowly, the two girls made their way up the gravelly path and stopped at the door. Silvia knocked lightly on the door.

Nothing happened.

Silvia knocked a little harder. When there still wasn't an answer, Silvia reached for the handle.

"No way, Silvi. That's how we got in this mess in the first place." Manuela grabbed her hand and pulled it back forcefully.

"What are you talking about? 'This mess?'" Silvia asked accusingly. "I thought you agreed what we are doing to help save the DragonFly Keeper and the magic of the world was a good thing."

"It sounded very important at Miss Sasha's. But we haven't done anything to help her have we?" Manuela turned and leaned her back against the door, crossing her arms for emphasis. Unexpectedly, the door swung in and Manuela fell backwards into the hut. Startled, she stood up and looked around her. Silvia had already walked in, ignoring her. It was beautiful. Sunlight poured in through the open windows and swirled around with the wispy smoke and bread smells coming out of the little stone oven in the back. Smooth gray stones made up the floor, with the wooden walls oiled a dark brown. But what made it beautiful to the two hungry girls was a little table that held a giant wicker bowl of apples, pears, plums and peaches; a smaller stone bowl full of cracked walnuts, hazelnuts and other nuts they didn't recognize; slabs of some juicy warm meat, some black mushrooms sautéed with sweet butter; and a giant pitcher of red juice.

"Oh, Manu, it's a miracle," Silvia said sitting down on one of the little wooden chairs and filling the empty plate in front of her with some mushrooms with the big silver spoon laid next to the bowl.

Manuela couldn't believe it. "Silvia! What are you doing? You can't eat that food!" She just stood there watching Silvia eat the mushrooms.

"Why not?" an older voice said behind her, "It is for you girls after all." Manuela spun around. A tall lady with a long blue skirt, a red blouse and a white apron stood in the doorway. Her blonde hair was graying but it only added to the luster of it as it swept up into a loose bun on her head. She had blue eyes the color of the frothing river, and she was smiling a small quiet smile. In her hand, she held some herbs and on one arm, a basket filled with fresh lettuce.

"You knew we were coming?" Manuela still stared at the woman's churning blue eyes. They seemed to be speaking to her in words she couldn't understand. Finally, unable to take the intensity, she lowered her eyes to the ground. When she looked up again, she saw that the woman was walking over to the oven. Silvia was just finishing the bite she had taken before the woman walked in. She stood up and stammered.

"I … Uh, I mean … we didn't know what … I was so hungry I didn't think … Please, don't be angry." Silvia said as she watched the woman pull out a steaming brown loaf that smelled better than anything Manuela could think of at the moment.

"Now, why would I be angry?" the woman said like a soothing grandmother. She placed the warm bread on the table and motioned for the girls to sit. "Eat first; then talk."

Manuela and Silvia sat down and the woman piled their plates high with the rich foods. She filled her plate next and started eating. Juice was dripping down Silvia's chin from the meat she was chewing, but no one seemed to care. Using a heavy silver knife, Manuela piled a slice of the bread with creamy white butter and bit into it. Her body shivered. Next, the woman poured a tall metal cup of red juice for each of them. Silvia drank hers eagerly while Manuela took a sip to try it first. Sloshing it around she decided it was like sweet grape juice with something else she just couldn't place. The woman watched them through it all taking small bites and sips.

When they were finished, Manuela suddenly remembered Fritz. "Oh, no. We have to go back to get our dog. He's hurt and we need to get back upriver before night." Manuela began to stand up.

"So that is where your companion is? Take heart. I will send Leo to get him." Rising gracefully, the woman whistled and a tall man with the same gray-blonde hair and a blue tunic came to the doorway. "Leo, take the boat and retrieve the poor dog so these girls can rest tonight." Pulling his cap, the man didn't say a word, but turned and walked out the door. "Don't worry, he will have your dog back shortly and we will take care of him ourselves."

"Thank you so much for everything. But how did you know we were coming?" Manuela asked carefully.

"That is not important. Now let us introduce ourselves. I am Davina. That was my brother Leo. Who are you? And what are you doing in the wood?" Davina looked at Silvia with her penetrating eyes.

"I … I'm Siliva. That's Manuela. We are trying to …"

"We are trying to find someone," Manuela interrupted swiftly. She smiled at Davina, but lightly kicked Silvia under the table.

"You are? And where are you going to find this someone?" Davina had turned her sweet smile and deep gaze to Manuela.

"Um. Well, we aren't exactly sure where. We thought we would figure it out on the journey." Manuela wasn't going to let too much information out if this was only a friendly and curious person. The contact should know what to say, if their experience with Aru had taught them anything.

Davina smiled as she cleared the table. "You are right to be cautious of strangers. How can I help you?"

"Well, where are we?" Silvia asked abruptly. Manuela glared at her while Davina's back was turned. Silvia just glared back. *Why can't she just be quiet! If we let her know we don't even know where we are, she is sure to know something is off,* thought Manuela.

"Of course, you are strangers to the wood. I could tell by your dress. You came from far away, I am guessing." Davina left the dishes in a large wooden basin and came back to the table with some biscuits. "You are in Latgale, in Latvia. We live alone in the wood because it is more peaceful. Does that help you, girls?" She brought over a glass jar of dark golden honey and layered the biscuits and handed one to each of them.

"Thank you, yes it does," Manuela said quickly. *Latvia? Where was that anyway. Maybe Europe. Yes, up by Norway and the reindeer.* Manuela had always liked social studies and now it was paying off. "And thank you, again. This food is wonderful. I don't know what we would have done if we hadn't found you." Manuela took a bite of the honeyed biscuit and let it melt in her mouth. It was so sweet and warm. She felt the tension of the day start do drain away. Strangely, Silvia didn't touch hers.

Just then Leo walked in carrying Fritz. Silvia jumped up and ran over to them.

"Fritz! I am so glad to see you! Are you O.K.?" Silvia stroked his ears and gave him a hug. Leo put Fritz down on a cushion that Davina had put on the floor when they walked in. Fritz licked Silvia's face and wagged his tail slightly. Manuela went over and bent down next to Silvia and Fritz.

"His leg doesn't look swollen." Manuela touched the makeshift bandage. Fritz moved his leg at the touch but didn't yelp. "Look, Silvia. It probably isn't broken, just badly torn up."

Leo looked down on them quietly. "Boar got 'im," he said in a low voice. Then he walked over to a cabinet and brought down some bright yellow ointment in a clear jar and some white bandaging.

"How did you get there and back so fast! It took us hours just to get one way." Silvia looked up at the tall thin man as he opened the ointment and then bent down to unwrap Fritz's bloody rags.

Davina chuckled softly. "Oh girls. How can you ask such questions?" she asked. "You yourselves appeared out of nowhere wearing those old rags and carrying those dirty packs. Perhaps we have something in common?" Davina winked at them as she motioned for them to come over to the table. "Now, let's let Leo do his healing in peace. You will see. Fritz will be as good as new by nightfall." Silvia and Manuela reluctantly got up and moved back towards the table. "Then you can continue your journey to 'somewhere'. But first you all need to rest. In the morning the woods will be less dangerous." Davina gave a big smile and her eyes seemed to bubble.

"I would like to wash these old socks now, Manu." Silvia said. "If we go down to the river, then maybe we could wash up." Silvia looked at Davina questioningly.

"Of course. Not only that, but I have some new clothes for you to wear. You can't possibly go around in those ripped up skirts and clunky boots." Davina glided over to a wooden chest under one of the red-curtained windows. Opening it with a creak, she pulled out two tunics, a gray one and one a midnight blue. Then she pulled out two pairs of black leggings and some thick brown leather slipper shoes and handed everything to Manuela. "These things should be much more comfortable, and I have no more use for them" she said with a smile.

Manuela took the things and followed Silvia down to the riverbank. They took off their boots and socks and the moss was soft and cool on their bare feet. Silvia looked back at the house.

"Something's not right, Manu," she said softly, turning back to look at the older girl.

"What do you mean? They gave us food and helped Fritz. They know who we are and that we were coming, even if they won't say how." Manuela stuck her feet in the river. It was just cool enough.

"I don't know. I know they helped us, but where is the castle?" Silvia asked as she waded in after Manuela and bent to splash water on her face.

"Come on, Silvi. Just because you *think* you remember some talking rat say something about a castle doesn't mean that is where the contact is supposed to be. Maybe that is where Shatru is keeping the DragonFly Keeper."

Silvia crouched down and dunked her head under, scrubbing at her curls. Finally, she came up and wiped the water from her eyes. She stole a glance back at the hut and then shivered. "Don't you feel it, Manu? In Aru's house I felt, I don't know, good." She started back up the bank. "This place is different."

"Of course it's different," Manuela said getting angry. "We are in *Latvia*. Do you even know where that is? It's probably as far away from Bolivia as you can get." Manuela splashed water on her face and arms. "Just let me decide what to do. I think we should ask them if they know about the DragonFlies," Manuela said.

"What?" Silvia had already changed into the new clothes and was tightening the leather strap that was around the gray tunic. "You just kicked me in there because I asked where we were and now you are just going to march in there and tell them what we are doing?" Silvia stretched the slippers over her feet and began tying back her hair with some leather string she found in the tunic's pocket. "You just have to be in charge. We are supposed to be in this *together,*" Silvia said angrily. "Let's just wait to see how Fritz is in the morning and then keep on walking downstream." Silvia held out her hand. "And how about giving *me* the *shaanti.* After all," Silvia said icily, "it will be my turn next to use it."

Manuela shivered. The air was turning cooler as the sun couldn't penetrate the trees in the late afternoon. The river was in shadow and her wet clothes were clinging to her. The hut beckoned warm and safe. She couldn't understand Silvia's paranoia. *She can't stand it when I'm right,* thought Manuela. *She can't ever think things through! If she would just stop going on hunches and be more practical we might actually get somewhere.* Manuela fished the *shaanti* out of the pocket of her ripped up skirt. It seemed so little and yet it glittered so beautifully, even in the shady light.

Silvia snatched the stone out of Manuela's hand and put it in her tunic's pocket. "At least wait until tomorrow morning to say anything, Manu," Silvia said.

"Fine." Manuela said climbing up the bank.

74

Chapter 8

Meeting the Rogs

BEFORE GOING TO SLEEP, Silvia went over to the corner by the door to check on Fritz again. He looked up happily and licked her face, wagging his tail. His wound seemed not to bother him at all anymore; whatever Leo had used was definitely magical. *But I still don't trust them,* thought Silvia. *If they were our contacts, then they would have told us by now. Aru said time was really running short.* Silvia smiled at Fritz. "Don't worry, boy, we will be O.K." she said softly.

Silvia stood up and looked over at Manuela sleeping soundly on a quilt by the cupboard. After coming in from their baths, Davina had offered them more biscuits, piling them with dripping, sticky honey. Manuela had accepted eagerly, and Davina had given the two girls a 'night-time' tea to 'calm' them for sleep. Well, Silvia hadn't felt like eating or drinking. She had smiled when Manuela had said that Silvia definitely didn't need help 'calming' for sleep. But now Manuela was out like a light. Davina and Leo said that they would sleep in a root cellar not far away.

Walking to the window next to the door, Silvia peered out of the sash. The dark forest looked very scary and overwhelming. But she had made up her mind; she knew she was right, and Manuela seemed to be drugged to acceptance. She made her way over to the cupboard and gingerly stepped over Manuela. Opening the door, she spied the yellow ointment. *Who knows when this will come in handy,* she thought. Nothing else looked familiar. Earlier, she had put some bread in her pack along with some nuts she found on a shelf back by the stove.

The light was very faint. No moonlight filtered through the tall pines and oaks. Trying to be quiet, Silvia grabbed the ointment and stepped over Manuela but landed on something hard.

"Owww!" screamed Manuela.

"Shhhhh! Sorry, sorry!" Silvia bent down and tried to put her hand over Manuela's mouth.

"What are you doing?" Manuela asked loudly. She batted Silvia's hand away and sat up rubbing her wrist. She noticed the ointment in Silvia's hand. "Is something wrong with Fritz? Davina said Leo would have him healed by nightfall."

"No, he's fine," Silvia said quickly. "Manu, we have to go." She didn't say anything else, just walked quickly to her pack and put in the ointment.

"You're kidding, right? We agreed that we would talk to the Healers in the morning," Manuela seemed to wake up immediately.

"Manu, I know you think you are always right, but this time *I'm sure.*" Silvia buckled up her pack and patted her leg. Fritz trotted over without even a limp. "You have to trust me. Please. Miss Sasha said we had to work together for this quest."

"That's right, Silvia." Manuela said quietly. "But you don't seem to know how to do that. Do you remember what happened the last time you ran off into the night?" Her tone was hard and her eyes were dark.

"Manu, don't you understand that you have been trusting them without question ever since Davina's honey biscuits and tea?" Silvia stepped towards the door. "I'm sure they drugged you somehow."

"Oh, please, Silvi." Manuela said with a stiff laugh. "I'm not coming. How far do you think you'd get in that black night, anyway?"

"Manuela," Silvia said slowly, "I hate to put it to you this way, but I have the *shaanti,* and you aren't getting out of here without it. So you'd better grab your pack and follow me. Now." Silvia opened the door and slipped out of the crack. Fritz hesitated, but, whining softly, he put his head down and shuffled after her.

Silvia took a sharp intake of breath at the cooler air. Inside the hut, the stove had kept the girls warm. *Well it sure isn't like Lake Titicaca,* thought Silvia. *At least here you can't see your breath when you talk.* Silva looked back and watched the door close. No Manuela. Her stomach tightened, and she almost went back in. *No, I can't give in. I must be strong.* Reaching down, she felt Fritz beside her and quickly wiped the tear that started down her cheek.

Following the path, but going slowly, she made her way down to the river. The moonlight drew a silver line down the gurgling inky water. It was only a crescent moon and shed little light. She began to pick her way downstream.

Suddenly she saw light all around her. "Going so soon?" said a smooth voice behind her. Silvia froze. She knew it was Davina. "It is quite dangerous out in the forests of Latvia, especially when you are *all alone*." When Davina spoke the last two words, her voice seemed to get lower and muffled. Curious, Silvia turned around. What she saw almost made her scream, but she clamped her hand over her mouth before that because she almost felt like vomiting. Davina was there alright, up the bank, bathed in a greenish light. But her face was not her face. Coming out of her mouth were tons of worms. Her eyes were all white and her arms were spread wide. The worms dropped down and began wriggling down to Silvia and Fritz.

Fritz squealed and started down the river. Silvia suddenly found her legs and began backing up slowly, afraid to look away from the frightening woman. When she heard a sharp yelp, she turned around and saw that Leo had Fritz in a big burlap sack. His eyes were churning like a green storm and he had a smile on his face. Silvia was trapped.

Jumping into the river, she tried to run downstream past the tall, thin man. He strode in the water and grabbed her by the hair, yanking sharply.

"Owww! Let go of me you disgusting ghoul!" she shouted, trying to hit his arm.

Leo bellowed like thunder and yanked again. "Come with me," he said in an unnaturally low baritone. "We will see what Sarpa will do with you. Now, Sarpa, we must go get the sister. Shatru distinctly said to get all the meddling up-worlders." Leo, or whoever he was, began pulling Silvia out of the river by her hair.

Silvia could see Davina, or Sarpa as Leo called her, up on the bank. While she no longer had worms coming out of her mouth, — and thank goodness they were nowhere in sight — her face had become a leathery black and her hair had shortened to a wiry, gray fringe. Her tall regal figure was now short and round and her hands were black with strange red bumps. As Leo pulled her closer, she saw that the intense blue eyes of the woman had turned a stormy green as well and had pupils slit like a cat's.

Silvia shivered as the cool night air hit her wet legs. Pushing her towards Sarpa, Leo let go and waited. "Well, healthy young wanderer," Sarpa said in a low crackling voice, "What do you think? I'm sure I didn't enjoy being Davina-the-cook very much. Thought you could just skip away?" Sarpa stuck her face into Silvia's. Silvia stumbled backwards at the gruesome sight of the red-pocked face up close.

"Well, this one isn't going anywhere. Bring her with you, Maarnu," Sarpa said jaggedly. "Let's go get the other one."

"Manu! Run! They are …" Silvia began to yell until she felt a hard bumpy hand reach around and clamp over her mouth and pull her back. She tried to push away, but the skinny 'Leo' turned out to be a very strong 'Maarnu'.

Suddenly, the greenish tint of the light began to change to more of a teal. Silvia looked up and saw tiny blue lights circling them in fast overlapping routes. The DragonFlies! Sarpa and Maarnu started batting at them angrily. Maarnu dropped the burlap sack and Fritz jumped out and ran into the trees.

"Silvia! Hurry, get away!" Silvia looked after Fritz and saw Manuela in the shadows waving wildly. The DragonFlies were making a high piercing wail which almost drowned everything else out, including the strange curses of the two monsters. Silvia thought fast and jammed her elbow back into Maarnu's stomach. He lurched and let go, giving Silvia the opportunity to escape.

"Maarnu, you fool!" Sarpa shrieked as the DragonFlies batted at her ugly face. "After them! Shatru will feed us to the volcano for this!" she screamed. But Maarnu was completely covered in wailing blue lights.

Her loose curls flying, Silvia stumbled over the mossy ground as fast as she could and took off into the dark woods after Manuela and Fritz. It was a long time before she realized she could no longer hear the high-pitched wailing. Her heart was beating loudly in her ears, out of fear as much as exhaustion. Finally, when she thought she couldn't go on, she saw Manuela stop and bend over breathing heavily, leaning against a tree. Silvia stopped, almost bumping into her sister. The two girls looked at each other with tears in their eyes and then only hugged tightly. What had happened was too much for words. Fritz rubbed his back on their legs, panting.

After their breathing slowed, the night sounds of the forest began to sound more menacing to the two girls. The gurgling brook was gone. A loud *"Chi-chi-chi"* hummed all around them, and they could hear crackles as twigs broke from small animals scurrying in the dark.

"Oh, Manu, what happened back there?" Silvia held her sister's hand as they both leaned up against the tree.

"I … I'm sorry. I should have believed you. When I looked out of the window, I saw this greenish light and … and then Leo … I mean Maarnu, grabbed your hair." Manuela closed her eyes tightly. "I grabbed one of Aru's crisps out of the velvet bag and ate it. Then they came and I ran over to the woods and called you." Opening her eyes, she turned to Silvia. "We almost lost everything, Silvia. I almost lost you."

Silvia hugged Manuela. Manuela had never showed so much affection before. Silvia felt confused and guilty, but she did love Manuela. "I'm sorry too, Manu. I think you were right about me running off without thinking. That's two times you had to save me. It's just… Well, you wouldn't listen to me." Silvia looked down. She didn't want her sister to see the hurt that was still inside her. While she was glad that Manuela had saved her, part of her was angry that even though she was right, her sister hadn't believed her, but had only come around when it was proven to be true. And it was Manuela who had done the thing to save them both. Manuela always seemed to do the right thing at the right time. Whenever Silvia tried, her excitement got in the way.

Manuela didn't notice her sister's subdued tone. "Well, I guess that honey was a little strange after all. I did go to sleep awfully fast last night." She rubbed Fritz's head and let go of Silvia's hand. "I think we need to keep moving. If we don't, I am afraid these night noises will do me in," she said determinedly.

As the two girls and their dog marched onwards, big fat raindrops began to sprinkle out of the sky. Soon they were soaked through. And tired.

"I really need to take a rest, Manu," Silvia said yawning. Dark wet curls were plastered on her cheeks and she felt itchy all over. "Let's just lie down for a little while."

"What if those … Rogs … come after us while we are asleep?" Manuela replied sleepily. But she knew that they couldn't keep it up for long. Fritz, though strong, was beginning to show a slight limp after the hours of walking. "Oh, alright. I guess we should rest before it is light out." Manuela and Silvia chose a soft mossy mound under the branches of a big fir that kept out most of the rain. Huddled together, the three fell asleep immediately.

Chapter 9

The girls get to know the wildlife

MANUELA'S HEAD THROBBED. She sat up rubbing her eyes, pushing Silvia aside. Tangerine light filtered in through the fir tree and misty air swirled around as the dew mingled with the morning sun. Soft as the moss was, Manuela's whole body felt cramped and achy. Whatever the Rogs had hidden in the honey was having its side affects. She glanced down at Silvia sleeping deeply, rolled up next to Fritz. What were they to do now? Sighing, she got up and crept out from under the tree to stretch.

The day was clear, and while her clothes were still damp, Manuela wasn't too cool. Looking around, she saw that this part of the forest was filled with larger trees than where they had come from. The trunks were thick and knotty with lichen and moss clinging to all parts. Big gnarly roots looped around the base of the trees hiding all sorts of different colored mushrooms. The mushrooms made Manuela remember her hunger.

"Manu?" Silvia's head popped out from under the branches. Fritz trotted out and began lapping up some dew that had collected in one of the giant tree roots. "Wow. It's so beautiful," Silvia said coming up next to her sister. The soft orange light peeked in and fell in rays across the dewy green moss and made it sparkle like a rainbow.

Suddenly Manuela grabbed Silvia's arm and pointed to the east, where the low light was coming in. "Do you see that?"

"What?"

"Look, it's a path, I think," Manuela said, pulling her sister closer to a certain patch of ground. Sure enough, when the girls got closer, they could see that the ground was trodden down and not as mossy. It led further east into the forest.

"Let's eat first, and then try it out," Silvia said opening her pack.

"Eat what? I'm not going to try those mushrooms to find out they are poisonous," Manuela said, rubbing her sore temples.

"Well, you don't think I would forget to pack *food* before I took off." Silvia smiled and pulled out the bread and nuts she had wrapped in her old sweater. Manuela looked at the brown bread and felt her mouth water.

"What if the food is tainted," she asked.

"I think they only drugged the tea and honey," Silvia said, munching on some nuts. "Nothing happened to me, remember." Manuela shrugged and sat down next to Silvia. She tore some of the bread and tossed some to Fritz.

After they cleaned up, Manuela and Silvia started down the path. Soon they began to see smaller trees under the canopy of the larger firs. The trees had a deep red wood and seemed to form a grove. Silvia stopped and pointed off the path to their left. Manuela saw what she was pointing to — a glade brimming over with beautiful flowers which wafted a perfume their way.

"Those flowers, they are so sweet-smelling!" exclaimed Silvia trotting over to inspect. Manuela couldn't believe she was just trotting off again.

"Silvia! Come back here. How are we ever going to find ..." She had been following Fritz and Silvia and stopped short when she reached the edge of the glade. Apart from the hundreds of colorful flowers, there was a very tall tree stump with a gigantic nest on top.

"That nest must be as big as a person!" She couldn't control her astonishment.

Silvia wasn't looking. She was sitting amid the purple flowers with her eyes closed smiling. When she heard Manuela, she looked up and saw the nest. She put her pack beside her and lay back with her arms behind her head. "Maybe it's a long-lost dinosaur."

"You mean, like a pterodactyl?" Manuela said quietly, shading her eyes for a better look. Just then, Fritz got up and began barking. Manuela saw it up in the sky circling and for a moment her heart jumped. The big white bird was huge, but it was no dinosaur. "It's a big stork, Silvia! Remember the bird we saw by the river?"

Silvia sat up and watched as the bird circled its nest and landed, paying no head to Fritz or the girls. Suddenly, Manuela heard a grunt coming from the edge of the glade. Turning, she froze; waddling out with its nose to the ground was an all too familiar big black hairy pig. Manuela tried to cross the glade slowly without making a sound. When Silvia looked at her, she put her finger to her lips to tell her to be quiet.

"What's wrong?" Silvia said loudly.

The boar looked up sharply and stuck its hairy snout in the air and then began to charge. Manuela frowned and ran the rest of the way to Silvia yelling loudly, "A boar! A boar! Run, run, run!"

The three travelers ran out of the glade and back to the path, taking the eastern route again. After a few minutes, Fritz stopped and the girls bent over panting. The boar was gone. Silvia pushed her hair out of her face and then stood up and her mouth dropped open. She was pointing to something behind Manuela on the path. Manuela's hair stood on end on her arms with fear, but she turned around slowly, unable to ask what could be there.

She let out a big sigh when she saw it wasn't the boar but the big stork, standing not three feet from them. "Silvia, it looks like its following us," Manuela whispered. The bird cocked its head at her words and marched closer. Fritz walked up to it cautiously and sniffed at its big scrawny legs. The stork didn't move. Then it walked right past them and turned off the path pausing about two yards out to turn around and cock its head at them again.

"I think it wants us to follow it," Silvia said quietly. Slowly the girls walked towards the stork with Fritz following. When they stepped off the path and started towards it, it awkwardly continued on until it came to a huge bright clearing. Running a little, it flapped its wings and soared into the air. Manuela, Silvia and Fritz ran to keep up. At the top of a rolling hill, they looked down and saw the stork fly into the loft-window of an old run-down barn.

"Well, *that* must be your castle, Silvi," Manuela said with a smirk. Fritz started down the hill towards the barn. "Let's see what's inside."

Silvia and Manuela arrived at the old peeling barn. It looked like it hadn't been used for a very long time; mold encrusted most of the rotten planks, and moss hung from the roof. Trying to look inside, Manuela found a loose board and pushed it aside as far as it would go. It looked dark through the cracks, and she couldn't see anything. Silvia walked over to the door.

"I don't know if it will open," she said as she pulled on the rusting latch. "It seems stuck in the ground here."

Manuela pulled hard at the door. Together they budged the door enough to squeeze through. Fritz went first, followed by the girls.

"I can't see anything!" Silvia said irritably. "And it stinks like bad cheese."

"Well, pull out your flashlight, then." Manuela already had her pack off and was rummaging around inside it.

Just then, the door banged shut behind them, leaving them in total darkness.

"D ... d ... did you just do that, Manu?" Silvia asked.

"No," Manuela whispered back.

"It could have been the wind," Silvia said hopefully.

"That door was stuck in the ground." Manuela found her flashlight. "O.K., Silvi. I found my flashlight," she said quietly. "I am going to turn it on and turn around at the same time. Are you ready?"

"No need. I'll just turn on the lights," said a tweedy voice. Immediately the barn was aglow with soft candlelight and the girls gasped. Instead of an old dirty barn, they were inside an enormous mansion. The tall walls were a cool blue and gray marble and had torches ensconced all along them. The floor was a pink and yellow marble covered in elaborately worked rugs in gold and blue. Sweet perfumed flowers, like the ones from the field, filled a tall porcelain vase on a red-wood table by the door. And the door! Manuela had never seen anything like it. It seemed to be made of pure gold with exotic markings worked in. Glittery jewels encrusted the surface like hard candies pressed in taffy.

Coming towards them was a small man in a formal black suit and a high white shirt with a ruffled collar. His white blonde hair was swept up in a great pompadour and swayed as he marched over to them.

"Mademoiselles Manuela and Silvia, I presume?" the little man asked in a formal tone. "*Labdien*, I am Sir Luta Bantavick. I was hoping you'd make it away from those dreadful Rogs. They do pollute the neighborhood a bit, I'm afraid to say." Sir Bantavick bowed to the two girls. "And you, my stout fellow, must be Fritz, their ever faithful companion. So good of you to help the Cause."

Silvia looked at Sir Bantavick and then Manuela. "The Cause?" she said slowly.

"Yes, yes. The DragonFly Keeper must be retrieved before it is too late." Sir Bantavick turned and began walking towards a doorway and passed through. "Come along. Food first as they say." And he disappeared around the corner.

"Now *this* is a castle," Silvia said smiling. "And he most certainly *is* our contact. She rushed to follow Fritz and Sir Bantavick. Sighing with relief, Manuela walked slowly after them.

Chapter 10

Meeting Sir Luta

SIR BANTAVICK'S HOME WAS NEVER-ENDING. They passed through hall after hall of marble walls and fabulous paintings. The paintings were swirls of aquamarine, sapphire, cobalt and shine, but Silvia couldn't discern what they were supposed to be. Ahead of her, Sir Bantavick was walking briskly and seemed to have forgotten about them.

"How do you do it?" Silvia called ahead.

"Oh, I do suppose it seems like a lot for just me, but I've gotten used to it and I actually enjoy roaming around for hours," Sir Bantavick replied.

"No," Siliva said a little breathless as she raced to catch up with him. "I mean, how do you make an old barn into a castle?"

Sir Bantavick stopped short and looked at her with his eyebrows raised. "Well, you don't think I'd actually *live* in an old barn, do you? It's just a doorway into your world. This is a castle, of course." He shook his head and continued down the extremely long passageway.

"My world?" Silvia looked up and ran after him. "But if you aren't in 'my world,' then where are we?"

"Hmphf," Sir Bantavick replied. "Ah, here we are!" Blocking their way was a pair of tall red-wood doors with giant ivory handles. Opening then with an exaggerated gesture, Sir Bantavick stepped back and let Silvia and Fritz enter.

The dining room was immense. Along the walls, myriads of candles protruded in silver candlesticks amid folds of gold drapery. Hanging from the red-tiled ceiling hung a gigantic chandelier dripping with glittering gems and shimmering candles. But best of all was the long wooden table down the center of the room flanked by at least twenty-two chairs. Its shiny red surface was set with huge silver platters heaped with delicacies. Sir Bantavick led her to a seat at the table that was set. A large golden bowl of water sat next to a green velvet mat on the floor.

"Fritz may prefer to dine here next to you," the small man said with a smile. Silvia was able to get a better look at him as they seated and waited for Manuela. His green eyes were large for his face and framed by lacy white eyelashes. His nose was slim and delicate, and his lips seemed carved from ivory. His paleness would have been unnatural except that everything was so unnatural.

"Sir Bantavick?" Silvia began to ask.

"Please call me Sir Luta. It takes less breath." Sir Luta sipped a small glass of water.

"O.K. Sir Luta, Manuela and I are a little worried that we don't have enough information to help do our part in this … cause." Silvia picked up her small glass of water and took a small sip.

"I understand completely," Sir Luta answered. "You must know that reaching me was the last test of your fidelity. Miss Sasha and Aru, wise as they may be, are not noble and, therefore, not permitted to know certain things." He looked up as Manuela came in and stopped in awe to look over the feast at the table and the sumptuous surroundings. "Miss Manuela. Please come and have a seat and we shall begin."

Manuela sat facing Silvia across the table. Immediately, Sir Luta picked up a tiny fork and chimed it against his water glass. From amid the golden drapery, a small wooden door opened and a line of men dressed in black formal suits and women in black dresses filed out and stood behind Sir Luta. He nodded at them and they began to serve. Silvia watched in fascination. The people all had white-blonde hair like Sir Luta and pale lips. But their eyes were all colors: green, blue, brown, even violet and gold. Without saying a word, they filled silver goblets with a dark honey-colored liquid and placed thick black bread on silver plates. Some forked out fat pancakes with cheese, while others spooned out ladles of a sour smelling stew of fish and vegetables. Even Fritz was served, which he thought quite amusing.

Silvia tried the stew first. Although it smelled sour, it was rich and appetizing. She looked over at Manuela who was sniffing the pancakes.

"Let me introduce you to my cuisine, ladies," Sir Luta said, laying his fork down and wiping his mouth with his white linen napkin. "First, you must taste my tomato salad. My chef, Zoja, is the best I've found yet. Her tomatoes are always the freshest." He inclined his head toward one teal-eyed maid, who spooned out a rich creamy mixture of chunky tomatoes with a large silver spoon.

"What are the green things?" Silvia asked.

"Why parsley and chives, child," Sir Luta said as he began to devour his salad. Silvia shrugged and took a bite while Manuela watched.

"Mmmm. This really *is* good, Manu." Manuela looked at Silvia suspiciously, but picked up her fork and ate as well.

Silvia couldn't believe the food. After the tomato salad, they were served warm baby carrots smothered in honeyed butter, nutty rye bread and a sweet cinnamon milk mousse with dumplings, which Silvia was *sure* was laced with samudra. The pancakes turned out to be made of potatoes and were heaped high with applesauce. After trying the sour smelling soup, Silvia decided that cod ball soup wasn't her favorite. Then servants piled their plates high with piragi, or dumplings filled with various meats and sauces like ham and mustard, beef and even bacon and rum. Sure that the meal must be over, Silvia sat back and sighed.

"Sir Luta, these dumplings are delicious! What's for dessert?"

"Silvia!" Manuela gave her sister a hard stare.

"Dear child," Sir Luta said shaking his head. "Dessert comes only *after* we've eaten our main courses."

Silvia looked at Sir Luta, puzzled. "Courses? But ... didn't ..." But before she could answer, Sir Luta snapped his fingers and the trays were removed from the table and immediately replaced with new ones with meat, fish and potatoes.

"I don't think I can eat anymore!" Manuela complained as she watched platter after platter of food being set on the table.

"Nonsense. In my dining room, you eat your fill ... and more. Now, see there. The problem is you haven't been sipping your sweet rhubarb juice." Manuela grimaced. "Come now. It has a touch of samudra and will give your stomach reserves you hadn't dreamed of before."

Silvia downed her third glassful and smiled mischievously across the table at Manuela.

"Here is my favorite, *karbonade*. These breaded pork chops will delight you!" Sir Luta almost shivered with excitement as he started cutting his cutlet. Silvia tried the pork chops and thought them delicious. When she next tried *aknu pastete*, she was surprised to find out that the mouthwatering meat with onions was fried liver. In between sips of the sweet rhubarb juice, they feasted on creamy baked trout, poached pike, fried sprats (which Fritz and Manuela passed on as soon as they learned they were sardines), herring with mushrooms and pickles and salmon roasted in dough. Finally, the servants cleared the table of their plates and the amazingly empty platters.

"But, I still don't understand *how* we ate all that food." Manuela said watching the servants retreat with the platters. "I mean, I don't normally eat that much fish, but I don't even feel full yet!"

"I should hope not. Dessert is yet to be served, and then tea of course." Sir Luta smiled and rubbed his hands together as the servants reappeared yet again with golden, jewel-encrusted bowls filled with puddings and pastries. After finishing some cinnamon apples and something called *debes manna*, or "heavenly manna," which was like cherry-flavored cream of wheat with vanilla Cool Whip, Silvia decided she was done. Unbelievably, she couldn't touch any more food.

After the dishes had been cleared and the tea served in steaming saucers, Sir Luta stood and motioned for them to follow him through a doorway to an adjacent room lined with plush blue sofas and gold-embroidered carpets. Walking carefully so as to not spill her tea out of the saucer, (who ever thought of drinking tea out of a saucer and not a teacup?) Silvia chose a particularly plump sofa and settled in with Fritz curling up beside her.

"Now for the serious part of our meeting. We have little time. Jiwan, the current DragonFly Keeper, has been located, but he is in the stronghold of Shatru and his Rogs. Hira, Jiwan's daughter, is currently organizing DragonFly warriors to raid the citadel. They have been unsuccessful, however." Sir Luta sipped at his tea.

"How are we to help then?" Manuela asked.

"Your journey is of the mystical kind, my dear. I only knew where to send you when I saw you in my hall. And as for where you go after that … Well, only the next contact in our chain will know this. What we all know is that the magic chain you travel, that Miss Sasha began, will end with your confrontation with Shatru. Your success will depend on your inner strength and your ability to trust each other."

Sir Luta finished off his tea and clapped his hands. One of the man-servants came and took his cup away and left a tray of small glass bowls filled with what looked like caramel covered vanilla ice cream.

"Is that ice cream?" asked Silvia, sitting up on the couch.

Sir Luta smiled. "Yes, of course. With a little Balsam on top; a Latvian treat to warm you before you go." Even though they both had eaten more than possible, they strangely felt hungry again and the girls each picked up a bowl and spoon, and Silvia put a bowl on the plush carpet for Fritz.

"Whoa," Manuela said, puckering up her face. She looked like she had sucked a lemon.

"Yes, yes, the first bite is a little surprising. Keep at it, though, and you will be well rewarded with strength and stamina later." Sir Luta's long white eyebrows flicked up and down as he talked and brushed up against the white hair fluffing out around his little head. Silvia thought he looked like a dandelion waiting to be wished upon.

Sir Luta's green eyes looked at Silvia and then Manuela. "Jiwan, the DragonFly Keeper, and his daughter, Hira, have been keeping the magic alive these past few centuries," he began. "It has been the hardest time in history for the DragonFlies to keep Shatru and his Rogs at bay. From their hidden grove they have sent out legions of DragonFlies to every spot on earth to spread nectar from the flowers that grow only in their grove. When the right person, usually a child, touches this nectar, that person's heart is filled with Jiwan's magic, a goodness that cries to be passed on through kindness and caring." Sir Luta paused to sip his tea. "Lately, Shatru has developed a way for his Rogs to change this nectar into something bitter and biting. When a person touches this changed nectar, they loose hope and dream towards despair."

"But why does Shatru want the DragonFly Keeper destroyed and people unhappy?" asked Silvia.

"Well, the fact is Shatru was once a Dragonfly Keeper Prince a long, long time ago." Sir Luta rubbed his little chin and closed his big eyes. "He had planned to be the next DragonFly Keeper but was passed over in favor of his younger brother Pujaa. Shatru had a different name then, but this I don't know. Angry, Shatru tried to steal one of the magic flowers in the grove's garden to go start his own grove." Sir Luta paused and opened his eyes. They were bright and gleaming, almost piercing. "When he cut its stalk, something never done before, the flower bled black nectar on him and changed him into the horrific creature he is today."

"Where is he now?" Manuela asked anxiously.

"When he saw what happened to his beauty, and that the flower melted in his hand, he fled the grove to an unknown place underground. Here he set up his rule and transformed unhappy creatures into ageless Rogs to carry out his revenge. He gets his magic from the nectar the dragonflies leave. Except that when he touches it, it turns into bile that stinks and causes sorrow." Sir Luta motioned for the girls to drink their tea.

Silvia fidgeted a little in her seat. "I've never seen any of this nectar. Is it like dew or something?" she asked.

"Oh, no." Sir Luta smiled. "It is ethereal; in other words, it is not for you to see, but to feel. Anyway," he said fluttering his lacy lashes, "the battle of revenge has been going on for all time, but now the balance is off. Jiwan, in an unprecedented attempt to heal the world, decided to take some nectar directly into the heart of Rog territory. He thought the strength of his magic could whither the sorrow and despair there." Sir Luta's eyes began to cloud over like giant raindrops. "But somehow Shatru captured him, killing thousands of loyal DragonFlies in the attempt."

Fritz walked over to Sir Luta and rubbed his nose into the little man's palm. Sir Luta smiled and wiped away a tear that had escaped.

"Why didn't he just kill Jiwan?" Silvia asked slowly. The sweetness of the ice cream and the strength of the liquor were beginning to have their effects.

"Power. Jiwan is supposedly the keeper of the Firestone. The Firestone is a key to a hidden magic reserve which can bestow the holder with amazing power. If Shatru gets a hold of the Firestone ..." Sir Luta looked down and rubbed Fritz's head. "Shatru is torturing Jiwan into telling him the location of the Firestone. But in time his greed for power will be overpowered by his lust for revenge. And then he will kill Jiwan and all the remaining DragonFlies." Looking into both girls' eyes he seemed to glow with a luminous energy. "If that happens, then your world will never be the same."

Silvia had to look away from the piercing gaze. She felt overwhelmed despite the calming effects of the doctored ice cream. How in the world were they to enter this magical, fantastically horrific world and free such a powerful being from such utter evil? She was tired and the constant excitement was having its toll on her. She felt like one does after a few days into a vacation in a strange place. Longing for her bed at home with the green and yellow quilt and the yellow walls and her colored pen collection, she closed her eyes. Feeling Manuela's hand on hers she opened her eyes and saw her sister smile as she squeezed her fingers. *How does she keep going?* thought Silvia. *She doesn't look tired or scared at all. How can I ever prove to her I am able to be responsible if I feel like curling up in a ball under my covers?* Silvia took a deep breath and finished off her tea in one big gulp.

"Thank you, Sir Luta. I think we have much more of a sense of purpose now. Our first goal is to find Shatru's lair," Manuela said confidently. Silvia sat up straighter, showing that she was ready for whatever came next.

"That leads us nicely to your departure, dear girls. I have a few parting instructions to give you before I send you off to your next destination." Sir Luta smiled and got up to collect their empty bowls and set them on a low wooden table beside the sofa. "Now I suggest you clean up and prepare to meet me in the rock room."

"Rock room?" Manuela asked as she tried to get up without falling over.

"Don't worry. Follow Lara there and she will show you the way." Sir Luta walked towards a closed door on the other side of the room. "Don't tarry. Jiwan awaits you."

Chapter 11

The Rock Room

AFTER WASHING UP, Manuela and Silvia followed a silent woman dressed in black with long white hair arranged in a bun on her tiny head. Lara led them down a long corridor lit with torches and lined with more of Sir Luta's fantastic paintings. She walked a good two yards in front of them, ignoring them completely.

"You still have the *shaanti*, right Silvi?" Manuela asked in a whisper.

Silvia put her hand deep in the tunic's pocket and nodded. Manuela sighed, trying not to look too relieved. She didn't want Silvia to get all touchy again. *But if we loose the shaanti, we are hopelessly lost and useless.* Manuela tried not to let her fear show.

"Silvia, remember back in Davina's cabin?" Manuela asked softly.

"You mean those disgusting Rogs. I don't know if I can handle that again." Silvia said. The girls walked on and on down the long corridor.

"Well, they seemed to know we were coming and tricked us. I think we should try to blend in a little more wherever we go next." Manuela tugged on her tunic. "Maybe change or something. We *did* get these from the Rogs."

Silvia nodded. "Yeah, let's ask Sir Luta when we ..." She didn't have time to finish. Lara abruptly turned and opened one of the many closed wooden doors they had been passing. She bowed her head and held the door open for the girls. Fritz, who had been padding along between the sisters, picked up his pace and slipped in ahead of them.

After walking in, Manuela stopped and stared. The 'rock room' was absolutely amazing. Each wall was tiled in five or six inch tiles of all types of stones. Manuela recognized marble of all colors and grains, granite, slate and even something that looked like lava rock. Silvia walked up to the nearest wall and ran her hand down the cool tiles. The floor was a swirling ocean mosaic made from all colors of pebbles that seemed to have been sanded down by the sea. Blue waves curled around gray whales and sharks with giant white teeth. But by far the most spectacular part of the 'rock room' was the ceiling; every inch of its surface was a shiny gem which let in light like a kaleidoscope stained-glass window. Purple, orange and yellow light streamed down from above them, giving the multi-textured and colored tiles a dreamlike glow. Manuela looked down the long room and saw a raised platform in the middle of the room. There, reclining on a blue and gold brocaded divan, sat Sir Luta waiting.

"Look, Silvi," Manuela said, reaching for Silvia's arm. "The light falling on Sir Luta makes his hair look like a clown's wig." The sisters giggled as they crossed over towards their host. Obviously, the effect of their 'strength-ening' ice cream hadn't worn off yet.

As they approached, Sir Luta smiled and rose from his seat. "You all look very refreshed," he said. Fritz came up to him for a pat. "Before you go, I have a few things for you. First," he pulled out a bright red feather from his pocket, "let me re-tone your clothing."

"You want to *what* our clothes?" Silvia asked with a puzzled look.

"Change their color and shape, my girl." Sir Luta touched the feather to the hem of Silvia's tunic top and bit his lower lip. "Hmmm … I think an outfit in black for you with a skirt instead of pants." Immediately Silvia's clothes blurred and, when Manuela blinked her eyes to try to see more clearly, she saw that Silvia indeed was now wearing a fitted black t-shirt and a loose black skirt. On her feet were simple but rugged black shoes.

"Whoa, that feather would really come in handy when I'm late for school." Silvia felt her clothes to make sure they were real.

Sir Luta placed the feather on Manuela's tunic and said, "I think you would be demure in a burgundy and gold ensemble." Manuela felt the faintest of tingling and looked down at what seemed to be a cloud enveloping her. When the cloud cleared, she was wearing a long-sleeved maroon fitted t-shirt and a muted-gold skirt similar to Silvia's, although with some black embroidered motifs on the hem. She, also, was wearing a pair of simple but rugged maroon shoes.

"Thank-you," stammered Manuela, still shocked at the sudden change. "We had thought about asking you for some new clothes since the Rogs knew what we were wearing."

"Oh, it's not for hiding from them, my little lady. Oh, no. The Rogs can sense you with their eyes, many eyes, closed. No, these are so you don't draw too much attention to yourselves from the locals." He placed the red feather back in his pocket. "No use in dropping clues to the spies who will go running to Shatru and his Rogs." Sir Luta folded his hands in front of him and sat down on his divan. "Now girls, the *shaanti?*" he said.

Silvia slowly felt around her new skirt until she felt the round stone and reached into a hidden pocket. After she pulled it out, Manuela saw how it shimmered in the fantastic light of this unique room. Sir Luta nodded and then sighed.

"It was such a pleasure to dine with you girls. I hope to do so again at the close of this terrible war. For now, I will send you on your way to Stromboli." Sir Luta paused as he saw the girls look at one another. "Stromboli is an island off the north-east coast of Sicily, which is southern Italy. Basically it is a volcano. Before I give you the words for the *shaanti*, I will give you a gift and some advice."

Manuela felt her hands go sweaty. *A volcano? We are going to pop into existence on an island volcano? Stromboli. So that's where that sandwich gets its name,* she thought. She rubbed her hands on her skirt and adjusted the pack she had been carrying to bring herself back to the moment at hand.

"You will need to find a book, an ancient book, with a map hidden inside. I do not have this book but I know its name." Sir Luta leaned in closer fluttering his white eyebrows. His large green eyes seemed to pop out of his head and shone with intensity. "The *Tala Pahaad*, or book of under the mountain. Somewhere inside is hidden a map which will guide you to Jiwan." Sir Luta pulled a small brown leather pouch and motioned for Manuela to come forward. He placed it in her hand and then sent her back. Manuela held the small closed pouch wondering what could be inside.

"I have given you three things. A rare river pearl, an orchid bud, and a coin made from the rare red-wooded yew." He looked from one girl to the other. Manuela felt sweat dripping down the back of her neck, under her long dark hair. "The pearl is to remind you that beauty is in the eye of the beholder and can be found anywhere. It can shine and lead you to safe harbors in a time of need. The orchid bud is from a particularly spectacular purple orchid, those flowers you see everywhere. It is to remind you that wonderful things can and do blossom from small unspectacular things. When opened, this flower can put those that wish to harm you in a trance. Finally, the yew-coin." Sir Luta leaned back on his divan. Manuela noticed that Silvia was eyeing the little pouch with interest. *Thank goodness he gave it to me. It sounds too valuable to loose,* she thought wryly. "The redwood coin," Sir Luta continued, "is to remind you that things in life are not free, but must be worked for in order to be of value. This coin will give you one thing, anything, in a time of great need. You must only hold it together. In order to use these gifts, I have made sure that you must be working together." Here he paused to scratch Fritz behind the ears. "Am I right that working together is sometimes difficult for you two?"

Manuela flushed and Silvia frowned. "Well, we some-times argue over what to do, but we both remember Miss Sasha saying that we need to work together if we are going to save the DragonFly Keeper," Manuela said. "Right, Silvia?"

"I guess," Silvia said still frowning. Manuela gave her a stern look.

"My advice to you both is to remember a little better for the rest of the journey." Sir Luta raised his fluffy eyebrows at them and then sat up a little. Manuela looked at her feet.

"You must get to *Pizzo sopra la Fossa*, or the top of the volcano. There you will meet your next contact and hopefully find the map to Jiwan," continued Sir Luta.

"We need to find a book at the top of a volcano?" asked Silvia. "It isn't blowing up lava or anything is it?"

Sir Luta smoothed his black trousers. "Well, only a little every fifteen minutes or so. I'm sure you'll do fine. People live on this island you know. Call Fritz now, Manuela. It is time to depart."

Manuela swallowed, trying to get rid of the knot in her throat. She found she was too worried to speak calmly, so she patted her leg and Fritz came trotting over. *I hope Silvia is able to remember the words she will need. I sure couldn't,* she thought.

Silvia was holding the *shaanti* with her right hand, and now she grabbed hold of Manuela's hand with her free one. Manuela held on to Fritz's red collar. "You do remember the procedure by now, I assume. I will repeat the words over and over until you feel you are ready. When you nod, I will stop and you may speak them. Now," he smiled reassuringly, "until we meet again."

The girls closed their eyes. Manuela squeezed Silvia's hand tightly and felt her sister squeeze back. *"Portami dentro la bocca del vulcano ..."* Sir Luta began to intone the words for the *shaanti* in a sweet melodic Italian. Manuela knew some Italian from her parents; she and Silvia had been born there after all, and their parents spoke it constantly. Her heart raced when she heard Sir Luta's words. *Take me inside the mouth of the volcano? A volcano that squirts out lava? Is he crazy?* With her eyes squeezed shut, Manuela began to feel dizzy even before she heard Sir Luta stop and Silvia begin.

"*Portami dentro la bocca del vulcano,*" Silvia said in a quiet but earnest voice.

Chapter 12

Silvia runs off again

LANDING WITH A THUMP, Silvia snapped open her eyes in the humid air. She was looking out at the deep blue sea and a hot breeze was pushing her dark curls all around her face. Brushing herself off, she stood and adjusted her old pack. Manuela was rising next to her. Fritz was sniffing the air and circling.

The air smelled salty and fresh even though it laid on them like a heavy breath. Silvia walked a little until she realized she was at the edge of a cliff. She put her arms out instinctively as she felt her stomach lurch. Below her, around 150 feet straight down, black rocks jutted out of the ocean spray.

"Silvia, watch out!" Manuela was soon by her sister's side. "This doesn't look like a volcano," she said turning around. They seemed to be on a rocky black plateau with hardly a clump of grass. Silvia looked where Manuela pointed. "Look, Silvia. That looks like some sort of lighthouse."

"But, *that*," said Silvia, turning back around and pointing out over the blue waves, "*that* looks like a volcano."

Ahead of them a giant smoking gray mountain loomed out of the sea. It had a narrow strip of white houses where it touched the water and some green going half-way up, but the entire thing looked like the tip of a dark, hot iceberg jutting out of the sapphire sea. Silvia inhaled the thick air and licked her lips. The taste was faintly salty.

Manuela didn't seem concerned. "Well, aren't you glad we didn't end up inside of it like Sir Luta's crazy words asked?" she said. "I was a little worried there for a minute."

"Why would he send us into a hot volcano, Manu?" Silvia said with a snort. "I mean, we wouldn't get far that way." She didn't want to admit that she had been a little afraid of where they would end up. But now she felt the worry again. "But how are we going to get over there? It looks like we are on a tiny island, and the volcano is *another* tiny island." Silvia turned around slowly checking out the plateau. "Didn't Sir Luta say we had to get to the top?"

Silvia and Manuela stared out across the shimmering water. It was too far to swim, even if they could think of a way to get down to the water. The plateau island was *very* small and seemed uninhabited. Apart from the lighthouse, there was just scrub and birds.

"Well, I guess we better get over to that lighthouse and see if anyone there has a boat. I'm sure we can communicate well enough here; we are in Italy," Manuela said, heading off towards the tall white tower and cluster of buildings. Silvia followed a few steps behind. "Oh, and I think you should give me the *shaanti* now, so we will be ready to move on quickly." Manuela didn't even turn around when she said it.

Silvia fumed with anger. "You just don't think it will be safe with me, do you," she growled.

Manuela stopped but didn't turn around. "Come on, Silvia. You know you're not the most responsible one." She turned around with an exasperated look on her face. "If you would just admit it and stop acting spoiled, we could work *together* like we are supposed to and maybe get somewhere."

Silvia clenched her fists as she stood there. "Oh, so working together is doing everything you say because you are so smart and great," she yelled at Manuela. "If it weren't for me, we would still be in Davina's little cabin or worse."

Manuela stepped closer and held out her hand. "Come one Silvia, *you're* the one who needed saving from those disgusting Rogs, not me." She met her gaze and stood there with her palm open. "Why do you think Sir Luta gave his special gifts to *me* to carry?"

Silvia couldn't believe it. Here they were only *minutes* away from Sir Luta's warning words, and Manuela was already taking over! *She doesn't need the shaanti now. She can just wait until the last minute,* thought Silvia. Pushing her sister aside, she starting running wildly towards the lighthouse; tears tickled her cheeks as they slid down in the hot breeze.

"Silvia, wait! Where are you going?" Manuela ran after her sister as Fritz sprinted past her and caught up with Silvia.

"I'm going to find a way off this island. Why don't you follow *me* for a change," yelled Silvia without stopping. She ran around to the back of the first white building she came to and stumbled down a slope of black pebbles.

While she was getting up, she noticed some steep steps cut into the rock leading down. Glancing behind to make sure Manuela was following her, she started down slowly, holding onto the rickety metal railing which ran alongside. Fritz paced back and forth at the top whining quietly. Finally, he barked down at Silvia as Manuela came up behind him breathing loudly.

"Silvia! What are you doing? What do you think you're going to do when you get down there anyway?" Manuela bent over and put her hands on her knees to catch her breath. But Silvia didn't stop or turn around. She put one foot in front of the other and followed the twisting trail as it hugged the side of the huge rock island. The air was cooler as she descended into the shadow of the rock face and birds scuttled out of her way screeching.

Manuela sighed. Holding on to the railing, she began to descend. Fritz looked a little apprehensive, but when he watched Manuela turn around the first bend of the steep trail, he sniffed loudly and started down behind them.

As she approached nearer to the water, Silvia could see ahead that the rock steps gave way to metal ones. They were deep orange with rust and some steps had holes in which the black-blue water peeked through. At the end of the staircase was a rickety dock. *But what good is a dock with no boat?* Silvia's shoulders slumped as she realized that her mad dash was only going to show Manuela that, once again, Silvia hadn't thought through what her plan was.

She could hear Manuela coming around the last bend of the stone staircase, so she took a deep breath and carefully found her way down the metal stairs to the dock. Water splashed up casually onto the wooden deck leaving it coated in slimy green seaweed in places. The scent of salt

110

was even stronger here, and Silvia walked carefully to the edge inhaling deeply.

Fritz padded up next to her and nosed her palm. Reaching down, she pet him absentmindedly and hung her head as she waited for Manuela to say 'I told you so.' But after a minute or so of hearing only the soft roar of the waves and cadence of splashes, she looked behind her, puzzled at the silence. Manuela was there alright. She was sitting on the last of the metal stairs with the little brown leather pouch from Sir Luta in her lap. She was staring at the open sea.

"Go ahead, Manu. Say it. Say 'I told you so,'" Silvia said coldly. Manuela remained silent and just sat there fingering the little pouch. "Manu," she said suddenly, having an idea. *Sir Luta's gifts! We could use the coin to ask for a boat,* thought Silvia, feeling like she could now redeem herself in the eyes of her sister. "Manu," she said again, more animated as she walked towards the older girl. "We can use the yew-coin! All we have to do is ask it for a boat!" She reached down towards the brown leather bag.

Immediately Manuela swung it aside out of Silvia's reach. "What are you thinking?" Manuela said frowning. "We can't waste that gift on a boat. What if we need it for something more important?"

Silvia's eyes narrowed and she put her hands on her hips. "You mean, we can't use that gift on a boat because *you* get to decide what is important. Maybe you just don't want my idea to be the one that works," she said angrily. "Well, we are never going to get anywhere in time to help Jiwan if we don't get to the next contact *soon*." Silvia leaned forward and tried to grab the bag from Manuela's outstretched hand.

111

Manuela got to her feet quickly and ducked around Silvia, going out onto the dock. "Why can't you stop being a baby and actually try to *help*. Now we have to climb up all those stairs to see if someone is up there so we can find a boat," Manuela said with a grumble.

That did it. Running towards Manuela, Silvia grabbed her sister's arm and pulled at the leather bag with all her might. Suddenly, she felt her feet slip out from under her. Her rugged shoes had not been rugged enough to keep her balanced on the slimy planks and she felt herself falling forwards and sideways off the edge of the dock. In shock, she gripped Manuela's arm tightly, pulling her down as well. Before she could scream, she felt the warm dark wetness envelop her, and she closed her eyes.

Chapter 13

The girls learn to work together

WHEN SILVIA CAME RUSHING AT HER, Manuela knew that they would fall over the dock, but she had no time to do anything. After the initial shock, Manuela opened her eyes in the clear, though dark, water. She could see which way the light was coming and headed in that direction. But where was Silvia? Looking around frantically, Manuela saw a glimpse of black surging toward the light above, and she kicked after it furiously.

Manuela's pack was pulling her down and she could barely make it, but when she did break the surface and gulp down fresh air, she sank back down. Gasping, Manuela was trying to look around for something to hold on to, when she noticed she had floated some distance away from the dock but nearer to some large rocks jutting out from the side of the island. After a minute, Manuela had a hold on one of the rocks and turned to look for Silvia. The salty water stung her eyes and made everything blurry, but she could make out something swimming towards the same rocks she was anchored to.

As the something got closer, she saw that it was Fritz pulling Silvia.

"Silvia!" Manuela shouted, pulling herself up onto one of the boulders and throwing off her pack. When Fritz came nearer, Manuela pulled her sister, who was floating face up, as if her pack were a buoy. Fritz scrambled up after them, shaking out his fur all over the black rock.

"Silvia, please be OK! I'm so sorry I called you a spoiled baby." Manuela pushed Silvia's wet curls out of her face and bent down to feel her breathing. Silvia was still breathing, though irregularly. Lifting her upper body, Manuela got Silvia's pack off, turned her on her side, and began pounding her back.

After a few seconds, Silvia started coughing violently and curled up into a ball. Fritz leapt over and started licking her face.

"Silvia? Are you OK? Please answer me!" Manuela said shaking Silvia's shoulders.

"I'm ... O.K. ..." Silvia said in between coughs. "How did I get up here?" she asked as she sat up rubbing her stinging eyes.

"Fritz swam you over, and I pulled you up. I think there is a current which pulled us over here." Manuela still had a hold on Silvia's shoulders.

"I'm sorry," both girls said at the same time. Smiling shyly, they embraced and then laughed when Fritz started licking *both* of their faces.

"But what do we do now?" asked Silvia more seriously. She felt quiet and resigned after her uncontrolled anger.

"I don't know Silvi, but I do know I don't want to be here when night comes." Manuela let go of her sister and grabbed her pack. "Where is the leather bag?" she asked suddenly.

Silvia blinked and put her hands on her soaking skirt, trying to find the pockets. But she knew that it must have been knocked out of Manuela's hand when she pushed her into the water. Silently she buried her face in her hands. She felt like crying, but she was too exhausted to do it.

"Silvia, look!" cried Manuela. Silvia looked up and saw Manuela kneeling and peering over the edge of their rock ledge into the water. A few feet away, a few yards down in the crystal water, the leather pouch was clearly visible amid a forest of white corals and red anemones. "How are we going to get it?" she asked miserably.

"We *could* swim down and get it," Silvia said slowly, joining her sister near the edge. Manuela turned to look at Silvia. "Maybe if we go down *together*, we would make it."

Smiling slightly, Manuela held out her hand and Silvia took it. "We can do this. We just need to stick together. Ready?" Manuela turned to Fritz. "Fritz, we will be right back. Don't worry."

Taking deep breaths, the two girls fell into the water and opened their eyes. The water was as warm as bath water and as clear. Kicking in a rhythm, still holding hands, the girls made their way down towards the coral ledge. They saw golden starfish and sponges nestled in the skeletal coral, and they were amazed at the variety of sea plants and algae. Glowing red anemones with purple feathery tips reached out towards them, swaying in the blue water. But the beautiful sea became more menacing as they went deeper. The water rapidly turned cool, and just as Manuela reached out and grabbed the leather pouch, and their breath was begin to burst out of their lungs, a quick current pulled them down and further away from the rock ledge and Fritz.

Manuela panicked and began to kick wildly, her hair flying around her like dark brown seaweed. Keeping a good hold on her sister's hand, Silvia grabbed Manuela's shoulder with her free hand. Although they were moving swiftly away, they were now heading up and toward a light. Manuela stopped kicking, and the two tried to help the current along.

Finally, their heads broke the surface and they gasped for air. They were in a tiny cave with an opening far above them that let in the late afternoon sun. The walls were slippery, but had a few pale blue corals which the girls used to anchor themselves. When their breathing slowed, Manuela pulled up her hand to show Silvia that she had at least gotten the pouch.

"We did it. But this doesn't look good," Manuela said. The tiny shaft of sunlight lit up the cave just enough for the girls to see they were in the top of a bottleneck. Only about five feet in radius, the walls curved upwards and came inches away from each other, forming a tunnel only a rat could crawl through which led up to the sky. Below them, the current was pushing more water up, pulsing them as if they were in some sort of weird hot tub.

"Manu, if we don't do something quickly, we are going to drown. Does this constitute as emergency enough to use the yew-coin?" Silvia asked without sarcasm.

Pulling the coin from the pouch carefully, Manuela held it up to the light. Carved into one side was a ten-petalled flower with strange chain-like images ringing the outside of the coin. On the other side, a beautiful figure was carved spreading double-wings, as if half man, half dragonfly. The water gurgled up closer to the girls' chins.

"What do we wish for? A boat is not going to be any use now," Manuela said.

"Sir Luta said anything, right?" said Silvia. "Well, let's wish for a safe way to the volcano. That way we get out of here *and* solve the problem of getting over there all in one wish. We do only get one, remember."

Manuela really smiled at that. "Leave it to you, Silvi. O.K. Let's close our eyes and hold the coin together and wish for a safe way to the volcano. Ready?" Silvia reached up and closed her hand onto Manuela's with the coin between their palms. Their heads were pressed together at the narrowest part of the little cave.

"We wish for a safe way to the volcano!" both girls said in unison, squeezing their eyes tightly. As they waited, water began to rise to their noses, and as they took deep breaths, to their foreheads.

Silvia's heart pounded. *Nothing's happening! I can't believe nothing's happening. It can't end like this. It can't!* she thought as her breath began to run out. Finally, she couldn't stand it any longer. She opened her eyes and tried to push at the wall of rock. What she saw amazed her. Bright sunlight was pouring in two feet to their left, over a school of azure colored fish and bright orange-colored anemones. Tugging on Manuela's arm, she pulled them towards the surface.

"It worked!" sputtered Manuela. "We didn't drown!" She pulled herself up onto the rock ledge from which they miraculously had come from under. Silvia followed her and the two lay down to catch their breath.

"We aren't drowned, but we asked to get to the volcano, remember? It seems to me we are still stuck on this huge rocky wasteland. And what about Fritz and our packs?"

Silvia sat up. "We can't even see the volcano from this side, only some other island or something far off over there." She pointed as Manuela sat up too.

Then all of a sudden the prow of a little blue rowboat came around the corner. It had black, white and yellow stripes painted lengthwise near the rim and red all along the rim with bright red oars. A small dark boy rowed towards them staring curiously. Probably about their age, but much smaller in stature, he was tanned from the Sicilian sun and his sinewy arms pulled at the oars as if he were used to the labor.

Stopping in front of them, he smiled and then raised his eyebrows as he gestured with one hand for them to get into the boat. The girls looked at each other, astonished. Silvia shrugged and Manuela nodded to the boy, who put out a hand to help them get into the little skiff without toppling it.

"Volete un passaggio fino al vulcano?" he asked in good Italian in a soft sweet voice. Before the girls could answer in their absolute shock, they heard a bark from around the bend.

That snapped Manuela out of it, and she blinked and stammered back in her American-accented Italian, "Si, we need a ride to the volcano. But could we pick up our dog and our back packs first, grazie?"

"Si, si. Andiamo," the boy said softly smiling. Silvia grabbed Manuela's right hand and held on tightly. In her left hand, Manuela still held the little leather pouch. The yew-coin had disappeared.

"I'm glad your Italian is not as bad as mine," Silvia said with a laugh. Fritz barked again when he saw the two girls coming. The boy laughed when Fritz licked him profusely as he jumped in the boat, rocking it violently. Manuela pulled in their packs and he began to row around the island.

"Io, Alfio." He said as he leant back and pulled the oars inward.

"Hi, Alfio, I'm Silvia. This is my sister, Manuela," Silvia said in her halting Italian. "Thank you for the ride."

"Oh, that's OK. I fish out here near Strombolicchio, and then I head back to home always at this time." Alfio said with the earthy Sicilian twang to his Italian. "But you two were not fishing, eh? What you two doing out there without a boat?"

Manuela sighed and looked out over towards the volcano as it came into view. The sun was sinking behind the large black mountain. Red shafts illuminated the smoke wafting up from the caldera, giving the island a pink halo which glowed, making it some devilish angel. "Alfio, we need to get to the top of that volcano. Can you help us?"

"The top?" he asked softly, whistling through his teeth. "Si, I can take you there. But first I cook us some food. I have not eaten since morning and the hike will take us about three hours if you are strong." Alfio pulled harder on the oars as they approached the black sands of Stromboli. Manuela and Silvia locked gazes and then laughed silently when they heard Fritz's stomach growling from the bottom of the boat.

Chapter 14

Who is Alfio?

THE SEA WAS CALM AS ALFIO brought his little boat along the shore of Stromboli. Silvia and Manuela had been silent for the trip, thinking of all that had happened since they *shaantied* into this new land. Manuela felt the *shaanti* in her skirt pocket. After Alfio had begun the journey back, Silvia had handed it over to her without a word. Not wanting to start another argument, but glad to have the stone secure in her pocket, Manuela had accepted it silently as well.

Now as their new host rowed them closer to the volcano, Manuela felt guilty that she didn't feel more responsible for egging Silvia on back on Strombolicchio. *It really* would *be easier if she just let me make the decisions,* she thought. *After all, I am the oldest anyway.* Sighing, Manuela watched her sister's hair drying in the salty breeze, curls starting to fly in rhythmic tumbles. *Silvia, Silvia,* she thought. *I really do love you and your excitement. I guess we wouldn't be here if it weren't for you.*

Alfio jumped out as the boat started to scrape sand. Holding the boat he stood there waiting with a smile on his small face. "Tutti fuori," he said matter of fact.

"What? You want us to get out of the boat into the water after we just dried off?" Silvia whined, making a face.

"Well, he probably can't pull the boat ashore with us in it, Silvi." Manuela cautiously lowered herself into the warm water. It didn't even come up to her waist, and she had taken her sopping wet shoes and socks off earlier and tied them to her pack. Silvia followed, bunching her skirt up a little too high.

"Silvia! Pull that down! Didn't you see how Alfio turned away embarrassed?" Manuela said under her breath. Manuela tugged her sister's skirt down and into the water.

"It's *my* skirt and *my* legs. Anyway," she said loudly in English as she stomped to the shore, "he didn't see anything but my knees."

Manuela waded in behind her and collapsed on the black beach. The air was cooling off a little as the volcano cast its shadow over the group. Alfio had pulled the boat up the sand until it would be safe from the tides, and then grabbed a net from under the seat. It was filled with long silvery fish with bluish fins and bright blue eyes.

"Now we can go eat. Follow me." Alfio said when he came over to the girls. They watched as he headed off towards the green scruff which began as the black sand started to rise against the volcano. He didn't even look back as he suddenly disappeared onto some unseen track. Manuela stood up brushing off the tiny beads of sand which stuck to her legs like tiny black freckles, and finished tying her laces. Silvia, whose wet shoes and socks sloshed as she walked, followed quickly and quietly behind her as they tried to catch up with their interesting host.

"I still can't see him," said Manuela. They had found only one track in the brush, and had been following the many footprints which led up towards the summit. "Fritz, can you tell if we are on the right track?"

Fritz wagged his tail happily at Manuela and went to the grassy side of the trail to pee. Manuela rolled her eyes at Silvia. "Well, I guess we all have to go sometime," she said with a giggle. Silvia grinned a little but didn't really laugh. "Are you OK?" Manuela asked as they continued up the hilly trail. Silvia had been following about two steps behind and hadn't said much the half hour or so they had been walking.

"Oh, I'm fine," Silvia replied with a small smile. "I'm just hungry. And tired. I can't wait to get to Alfio's meal." Manuela shrugged. *Still, it's not like her to be so quiet, even if she is hungry and tired,* she thought. *Maybe she's trying to act older or something. Oh well, that won't last long.* Manuela's stomach was beginning to growl as well, so she decided being silent wasn't so bad.

Suddenly Fritz darted off the main trail and through a break in the ever-present bush. Manuela rushed in after him and then stopped in her tracks as she saw the little white stucco hut with smoke rising out of its chimney. Even Silvia smiled at the beauty of the little garden of palm trees and bright pink flowers which hung down a little stone wall behind the house. A stone table outside had been set with thick clay dishes in a deep glazed orange and little glasses filled with wine and water. In the center was a bouquet of yellow wildflowers in a blue glazed jug.

"I can't believe Alfio did all this; he looks like he's just a boy," Silvia said. Fritz wagged his tail and lolled his tongue about as he found a pool of water to sip from. Manuela was about to call him and turn back to the trail, when Alfio came out and placed a tray of cheeses and olives on the table. Instead, she just raised her eyebrows at Silvia and walked over to the table and sat down, putting her pack by her feet. Silvia began eating the cheese immediately and Alfio smiled at her appetite.

The meal that followed was one of the best the girls had eaten so far on the journey. After bringing out sesame biscuits and 'malmsey,' what Alfio called the "nectar of the Gods," he brought out salads of juicy oranges and lemons drizzled with dark green extra-virgin olive oil and white vinegar, slices of smoked swordfish — that Alfio claimed to have caught himself — topped with capers and slivered almonds. The girls soaked up the dressing with hunks of the warm white bread which filled a wicker basket. After the salad, he brought out a huge steaming bowl of spaghetti tossed with tiny round tomatoes which had been stewed with garlic, paprika and oregano. The steam rose through the ricotta heaped on top and scented the air with the invigorating scent of freshly picked basil.

Manuela thought she couldn't eat another bite, when Alfio returned from his cottage with a giant platter of the silvery fish, grilled and covered with lemon slices, capers and olive oil. Even Fritz licked his lips. Finally, when the fish was gone, Alfio brought them little pink deep-fried cakes dusted with powdered sugar. The 'pink' turned out to be warm wine. During the meal, Alfio ate little and mostly told them about the island and what he did there.

He lived alone, not really explaining why. Every morning he fished and twice a week he traded at the port for other necessities. His garden supplied him with everything else he needed.

"Don't you get lonely here all by yourself," Silvia asked, gaining back some of her old self with each bite she took.

"Not really. Many times I run into visitors, such as you." Alfio nibbled a bit of bread which he dipped in his malmsey. "I walk often up to the top to watch the red stone burst and run down the volcano at night."

Manuela took another sip of wine. Every twenty minutes or so she had heard a rumble and felt it under her feet. Remembering Sir Luta's remarks, she realized that what she was feeling were small eruptions. "It's not going to run down here, is it?" she asked quietly.

Alfio laughed. "It hasn't come this way for hundreds of years. I doubt it will now." Manuela gave him a strange look. *How would he know? He can't be more than twelve. Maybe he's making everything up.*

"It's time to go, now," he said more seriously. "We need the light we have left to get to the caldera. There is little moonlight that makes it through the smoky sky." He motioned for them to leave the dishes and, slipping his leather sandals on again and grabbing a big walking stick, he led them back onto the trail and up towards the top.

"Don't you want to know why we are going up there?" Silvia asked after they had been walking in silence for a few minutes. The whirring of crickets and other insects was loud and almost drowned out the crunch of their footsteps on the dark pebbles. Manuela tried to kick her sister, but missed and ended up stumbling sideways.

"Of course. But I think if you wanted to tell me, you would. So I just enjoy your company until we get to the caldera and then I will find out," Alfio replied with a smile.

He's a little too smart for a boy, thought Manuela. *I don't know any boys back in Cleveland who could cook a meal like that by themselves. And now he has to have a reason for taking us all the way up there.* She walked silently and nervously. What if they were walking into a trap of the Rogs? What if this little boy earned something for bringing them in? He sure could use any help he got living all alone.

Then Fritz stopped in front of her and she almost stepped on his tail. He stuck his nose in the air and then she felt the rumble and heard the boom of Stromboli.

"Look there," Alfio said, pointing ahead and to the left. "See the red river?" Manuela felt the hair on her arms raise in goose bumps as she saw the glowing red line they were heading to. She unconsciously rubbed her pocket where the *shaanti* nestled, trying to get rid of her fear.

"Andiamo," he said, and led them up across increasingly rocky terrain.

As it grew darker, the group had to crawl up boulders, side-step rust-colored lava trickles and endure ever increasing heat. At one point, after the path seemed to be near the top and made a sharp bend, Alfio stopped and pointed down to a vast hollow below them. "This is the 'Sciara del Fuoco' where Stromboli spits out pieces of her heart. Wait and you will see." He sat down on the edge of the path and crossed his legs, leaning his chin in his hands and gazed out across the sea.

Manuela was glad for a rest, and she immediately plopped down next to him, while Silvia curled up with Fritz. The minutes passed silently, and Manuela was sure Silvia was almost asleep when they heard the explosion, much louder this time, from behind them and then a giant boom coming up from below. She saw Silvia jump up startled when, as if a bomb went off, the ground below them spit up a shower of rocks and they heard them rolling down the hills in the near-darkness. Alfio waited until the only noise left was the crickets whirring, and then, without a word, he got up and continued on their trek with Fritz and the girls very close behind.

Soon the dark gray coils of smoke started to blend in with the sky until the night descended almost at once. Alfio soon had them rounding a bend that seemed to level off. Silvia was audibly panting alongside of Fritz, and Manuela didn't think she could climb much more.

"When are we going to ..." began Manuela. But she didn't get to finish. A loud deafening bang caused her to drop to the ground and put her hands over her head like in school tornado drills.

"Manu, look!" shouted Silvia. Reluctantly, Manuela peered over the crock of her arm and saw Silvia pointing to their right. Suddenly another bang went off. Rising into the black air, a fireworks display of yellow, orange and feathery red fanned out from a few central plumes. The ends of the feathery cones arched back and descended like hot glowing raindrops to the ground below. Manuela could smell a pungent outhouse smell and could barely see Alfio ahead because of all the smoke.

"Well, I guess we are at the top," she said as she hurried to catch up with their guide.

"Si. This is the *Pizzo*, where you wanted to go. At night, she is spectacular, no?" Alfio was standing and pointing to the strips of glowing red which snaked their way down through smoky rocks. "She has three mouths, see?" Alfio didn't have to show them where, the after-image of the three yellow explosions still burned in their vision.

"Why is it so smelly here?" Silvia asked wrinkling her nose.

"That's the sulphur. It's what makes the rocks yellow too. You can see that better in the day," Alfio said. He sat down with his back against a rock and smiled up at Manuela, who could barely see him in the smoky darkness. "So, what now?" he said in a maddeningly calm voice.

Manuela coughed. "We wait. We wait until we find what we're looking for."

"And might I ask, what is that you are searching for so that I can help?" Alfio asked in his swaying Italian. In answer, Manuela turned and walked over a few feet to where Silvia had sat down with Fritz curled up beside her. A loud hiss burst out behind the pair, which made them jump and Alfio laugh.

"Look, it is just more lava pouring from her lips. You will not see spit more lovely." Alfio continued laughing to himself as he settled in comfortably and closed his eyes.

"He sure is a strange boy," Silvia said quietly, peering over at the little figure who appeared to have gone to sleep. "'Lovely spit?' That's disgusting. And 'lips?' I mean, come on." She turned to look at the smelly rock she was leaning against. "Manu, it sure smells like we are in the 'mouth of the volcano,'" she said with a forced laugh. "So what now?"

"I guess we wait here until the contact shows up, or we find a library." Manuela said shaking her head. "Where does Sir Luta think we could find a book around here?"

Silvia yawned. Despite the crazy surroundings, Manuela could see that she needed to sleep. She didn't think she, herself, would be able to. After a few minutes of staring off into the smelly smoke and trying to figure out what the crackles and rumbles all around her were, Manuela turned to hear Silvia snoring, her head propped up on Fritz's back. Hugging her knees to her, Manuela tried to sleep, but the spookiness of the volcano wouldn't let her close her eyes. She wished that the DragonFlies would come out to be with them. It was for them, after all, that they were undertaking this insane journey.

Just then, she had an idea. Rummaging in her pack, she pulled out the little bag Aru had given them in Bolivia. Inside were two remaining crisps; they hadn't dissolved from their trip through the ocean. *What if I ate one now? Maybe the DragonFlies could help us find our way to the next contact,* thought Manuela. *Or maybe I can try to talk to one this time and find out more about Jiwan.* Manuela brought the wafers up to her nose and inhaled. The sweet scent made her mouth water in contrast to the foul smell floating around them.

A soft hissing sound startled her out of her thoughts and she pulled the bag shut and shoved the wafers in her pocket next to the *shaanti.* A loud explosion rang out and a gigantic plume of fire sprayed out one of the craters below. Manuela sighed and swallowed. She could see in the orange glow that Alfio was still propped up across the path, and Silvia only turned slightly. Fritz looked out at her with wide open eyes. His ears were pricked and he turned his head slightly towards the direction of the craters. Manuela was glad to have someone else awake.

Again the hiss sounded, and Fritz whined quietly. "It's O.K. Fritz. This volcano is full of danger, but I'm sure Alfio would not have picked this spot to nap if he thought it might rain fire." She reached over and patted his back leg. She was still amazed at how the healing herbs had so quickly fixed him up.

This time the hiss was louder and longer and definitely NOT coming from the craters. Manuela felt prickles go up her spine and saw Fritz's sandy hair stand on end between his ears. Fritz's lip curled up and his dagger-like incisors gleamed in the yellow glow as he growled into the darkness down the path. Manuela didn't take her eyes off the area from where the sound came as she tried shaking Silvia awake.

"Silvi, Silvi! Wake up now," she tried to whisper as loudly as she could. Her chest was squeezing her breath and making her voice squeaky. Then again the hiss came from the gloomy dark path, sharper and louder. Silvia was awake now rubbing her eyes.

"What's going on?" she said groggily. "Why'd you wake me up already? It's not light out." Silvia blinked at Manuela's white face. She glanced at Fritz who was standing now and still snarling. Finally, she looked down the path at where their eyes were fixed and heard it — many long drawn out hisses overlapping each other.

"Silvia, I don't think that is the volcano," Manuela said grabbing her sister's hand. "Why doesn't Alfio wake up?" she asked looking at the sleeping boy. He hadn't even stirred.

Fully awake now, Silvia grabbed her pack and rummaged around. "It sounds bad, whatever it is. Maybe something in here can help us" she said pulling out the black lei.

"What are you going to do? Welcome them to the island?"

Silvia didn't seem bothered by Manuela's sarcastic tone. "Well, I was thinking that maybe it had some special power. I mean, all these things are turning out to be magical. Maybe this is too."

"But that isn't going to help if we don't know *what* its magical power is." Manuela whispered in the dark. The hissing had gone, but Fritz was still snarling and staring.

"I think maybe we should wake up Alfio," Silvia said, holding the lei in her lap. "It's probably time he knows why we're here. What if they're Rogs?"

"You're going to have to do it, then," Manuela said squeezing her sister's hand. "I can hardly move."

Silvia slowly stood and unconsciously put the lei over her head. Quietly she tip-toed in the direction of the hissing, where Alfio was sleeping. When she was only a foot away, the hissing came back, and through the smoky darkness, Manuela heard Silvia scream.

Chapter 15

The girls learn who Alfio is

TIME SEEMED TO STAND STILL for Silvia. She was aware of the dark, the cool night air, and even the stink of the smoky yellow stones. But in front of her, reaching at least five feet off the ground, were three giant oily purple snakes. They had bulging yellow eyes the size of softballs and rows of shiny gray teeth. Impossibly long skinny blood-colored tongues flicked in and out of their slimy mouths. They were hissing softly now and swaying, as if they were in a rhythmic dance. Silvia had stopped moving after her scream and her bottom jaw was hanging there as she stared at the gruesome snakes.

In the background, she heard Manuela screaming and Fritz barking, but the loudest noise was the hissing. The snakes started sliding closer, their slimy bellies slurping over the yellow and black rocks of the path. Finally, Silvia snapped her mouth shut and blinked. She started to back up slowly and tripped, landing on her backside. That is when she noticed that Alfio was missing. *Where could he have gone? He was just here!* Silvia scrabbled backwards into the dusty scrub as the snakes advanced slowly.

Suddenly the largest of the three, the one in the middle, lunged forward and opened its wide jaw inches from Silvia's face. She couldn't even scream as she felt the hot foul breath of its hiss and saw its bulgy mucus-dripping eyes staring at her. Then a long gooey tongue licked her cheek. Almost immediately the snake shrieked and snapped back up with the other two. Leaning back on her elbows with her skirt caught around her knees, Silvia let out a loud sigh. Her body was shimmering gold in the black night, and the black lei had turned the brightest gold. The snakes circled around her now, but didn't come close again.

Then the large snake looked off in Manuela and Fritz's direction. Manuela had stopped screaming and was standing behind Fritz pulling on her hair. When she saw the thing swing her way, Manuela put her hands over her mouth trying to muffle her scream.

"Manu! Run! I think they can't get me because of this black lei. Run!" Silvia screamed loudly.

"Alfio," Manuela whined slowly. "They got Alfio." She didn't move. Fritz jumped at the large slithering snake as it made its way towards them. The snake reacted quickly, sinking his fangs into Fritz's back.

"Fritz, NO!" screamed Silvia, getting up and running to the yelping dog. As she approached, the snake let go and joined its companions. She got down and cradled Fritz's head. Blood oozed from two large punctures in his back.

"Silvia, they're coming! Silvi!" Manuela staggered backwards as the snakes began to slide in her direction. Suddenly Manuela reached into her pocket and pulled out one of the special samudra wafers from her pocket and ate it, chewing intensely instead of letting it melt in her mouth. She stumbled over their backpacks and fell to the ground, but when she tried to get up, she winced. Her ankle must have turned.

Silvia looked down at Fritz and then tried to move him, but he was too heavy.

"Manu!" Silvia screamed as she got up and ran after the snakes. "Manuela, the DragonFlies!" she gasped stopping in her tracks. Swirling into the air all around Manuela was a blue mist full of sparks. The snakes stopped. Twirling in agitation, they opened their large maws and hissed a low throaty hiss. Silvia stepped back slowly to Fritz in fear at the sound.

The scrub rustled, and just then a big boom went off from the volcano and the fiery hiss of hot lava spurted into the sky. The red light bursting in the air lit up the surrounding grasses and what Silvia saw made her scream despite herself. Hundreds of snakes were lifting their black and yellow and red and green heads up out of the scrub and slithering towards the path. The purple snakes seemed to cower in a green glow from the gold of Silvia's shimmering and the blue sparks which were building up around Manuela.

Just when Silvia thought they were outnumbered, the DragonFly sparks started shooting out into the field and slashing into the myriad of snakes there. The Purple Monsters, as Silvia had begun to think of them, stopped their horrific lullaby and turned their eyes on Manuela who seemed unnaturally calm and still in the middle of the blue cloud. Screeching, they lunged at her, only to get caught by a spark and recoil back. Silvia actually wrung her hands trying to think of a way to help. *What is it about this lei that they don't like?* she thought.

Suddenly, Silvia had an idea. Sir Luta's orchid bud! She remembered he had said that it would put their enemies in a trance when it bloomed! Running around the Purple Monsters, Silvia grabbed Manuela's pack. Her gold glow enveloped the pack as she touched it. Glancing back at Fritz, she saw that the snakes were leaving the prone dog alone, so she turned her attention to finding the little leather pouch. Finally, she found it and grabbed the little bud and lifted it out. It was closed in tightly. *Now what? It isn't going to help if it won't bloom,* she thought. She could feel the heat from the sparking blue cloud, but the DragonFlies were not visible to her. Manuela looked off into the distance as if she were listening to a song.

Breathing deeply, Silvia knew what she had to do. Sir Luta had said that the gifts would only work if they were *together*. Shielding her eyes, she ran into the cloud, feeling the hot prickles, just missing the dripping fangs of the swollen snakes by a few inches. Grabbing Manuela's wrist, she leaned close to her ear and yelled. "Manuela! I need you! Manuela, please!"

Blinking, Manuela seemed to jerk as she turned and saw Silvia holding the orchid bud close to her face. "Manu, we need to open this bud together. We need to think it open together!" Silvia yelled above the hissing of the snakes and the howl of the windy cloud.

Manuela nodded and grabbed Silvia's other hand closing her eyes. Silvia did the same and envisioned the field of orchids back in Latvia, willing the bud in her hand to open up. Suddenly the hissing stopped. Silvia opened her eyes and saw through the cloud that the snakes' mouths were shut and their eyes were staring at the beautiful lavender and violet orchid in her hand. The blue cloud crackled and then the sparks all flew off into the fields into the remaining snakes, now silently staring. Then they were gone and the sudden silence was shocking.

"It worked, but now what?" Manuela said looking at her skin glowing gold from touching Silvia. "We should get to Fritz and find Alfio." She said, answering her own question. Reluctantly letting go of Silvia, Manuela walked in a large circle around the staring snakes, and over to Fritz. Silvia took slow steps in the same way, but the snakes eyes seemed to follow her so she stopped.

"Manu, find Alfio! I'm not sure how long this flower will work!" Silvia said a little loudly in the silent night.

"I can't see anything! Maybe if I get the flashlight ..." Manuela started to say. Just then a big boom and spray lit up the smoky ridge and Manuela could see Alfio lying on his back a few feet from the path. "Silvi, he's been bit too," she said when she reached him. Silvia didn't respond. She couldn't take her eyes off of the slobbering things in front of her. The longer they stayed still the more her terror built that they would suddenly wake up.

Manuela ran over to Silvia's pack and grabbed the ointment Silvia had taken from Davina's house in the woods. First she stopped at Fritz to lather it on his open wounds, and then she ran to Alfio. She found two smaller fang marks on his wrist and rubbed him with the rest of the bottle. She lifted him and carried him over to Fritz and sat down between them.

"Silvia, you have to come here. I don't think I can move Fritz. They both seem to be breathing." Manuela waited. "Silvia? Did you hear me? You have to come over here." Still nothing.

Silvia wanted to answer. She wanted to move. But she couldn't. Her voice seemed caught in her throat and she couldn't keep her eyes from the slitted eyes of the huge snake in the middle. It was if he had her locked in a trance as well. Finally she closed her eyes.

"Manu. I can't move. I'm afraid if I open my eyes and see … them …, I won't be able to talk again." Silvia kept her eyes shut tightly.

Just then Alfio began to stir and he sat up blinking. "Alfio! We're so sorry. I … don't know what to say first." Manuela stammered as Alfio rubbed his wrist and inspected it and the purple monsters.

"Silvia, you need to open your eyes and walk over here now," Alfio commanded in his young but very stern voice. "Leave the orchid on the path there."

Immediately Silvia opened her eyes and, after slowly placing the beautiful flower on the ground, sidestepped around the snakes. When she reached Manuela, Alfio and Fritz, the snakes were all still absorbed with the orchid. She opened her mouth to speak, but instead kneeled down beside Fritz and hugged him closely.

"Do not worry about explaining. I am what you have been searching for," Alfio said calmly as he placed a hand on each of the girls. "Now that I know you are ready for battle, I can send you on your way. We must hurry before the flower fades." With that, he got up and motioned for the girls to follow. Fritz stirred in Silvia's arms and turned to lick her face.

"The marks are still there, see," Manuela said to Silvia, pointing to Fritz's back, "but they are already so much smaller. I think he'll be O.K."

The girls got up and grabbed their packs and pulled out their flashlights, all the while keeping an eye on the large snakes and the flower. Striding purposefully, Alfio led them further down the rocky path. When they were walking briskly for almost five minutes, the path began to slope downwards.

"Alfio," Silvia panted trying to keep up with the boy. "If you were our contact all this time, why didn't you just tell us? Why let us get into this mess in the first place," she said angrily.

Alfio stopped and turned to her, causing Manuela to bump into Silvia. "Don't you see? This 'mess' as you call it was a battle. The three of you won against the magic without my help. The battle was a test." He began walking again, taking lunging steps as he moved down the slope. "I didn't know what the test would be, only that I needed to wait to see if you could continue."

"But you could have been killed!" Manuela said in confusion. "And we could have been killed," she said more quietly.

"But I wasn't. And you weren't." Alfio stepped off the path and the girls followed him until he stopped. A loud boom announced another plume of fire and Silvia gasped when she saw the landscape lit up with the Halloween glow. Below them began the 'sciara del fuoco,' the almost black vertical slide which carried all the volcano's blasted rocks to the sea. It began about twelve inches from where they stood.

"There is no time. Where is the *shaanti?*" Alfio said without a smile. He waited while Manuela brought out the smooth stone. Its golden specks seemed to shimmer in the fading red glow.

"What about the map?" asked Silvia. The glow from her lei had stopped long ago, and now she placed it in her pack as she spoke. "Sir Luta said we would need a map to find Jiwan. In a book, I think. We need that map, Alfio."

"Ah, yes." Alfio frowned. He seemed so much older than a boy of twelve in that frown. "But I know of many maps. Which map is your map?"

"The *Tala Palad* or something, I think it was," said Manuela quickly. "He said it was hidden in there."

"Oh, yes." Alfio smiled. "The *Tala Pahaad*, the book of the mountain."

"Yes! That's it!" exclaimed Silvia. "How do we get it?"

"When you get to where you are going, you must find the answer to this riddle: *I am old and drooping too, but every year I'm new. Give me the gift that I love most, and I will give to you.*" Alfio stopped and kept his smile. "I'm sure that you and your dog will help us in our quest for the DragonFly Keeper." He held out a big giant lemon to Silvia. "This is a cedro. It is from my own garden. I have had it for hundreds of years." He smiled as he saw the girls' eyes go wide. "It was from a tree that was once in the DragonFly Keeper's garden. That tree has long since gone, but I have a few of its fruits still." Silvia took the large cedro. "Using the juice of this fruit will enable you to understand the language of Shatru and the Rogs. Use it wisely."

Manuela grabbed Silvia's hand after Silvia had put the cedro in her pack and put it over her shoulder. She glanced behind them and clutched the *shaanti* with her right hand. "Where *are* we going, Alfio?"

"Into the heart of darkness," he smiled. Manuela and Silvia didn't smile back. "You are going into the Congo Basin. Into the darkness of the jungle of Africa. But don't worry. Once you solve the riddle and get the map, you will know how to go the rest of the way." Alfio crouched down next to Fritz and scratched his ears. "Look after your friends, brave one," he said softly.

Straightening, he instructed Manuela and Silvia to close their eyes and waited until they did. Without bothering to say goodbye, he began chanting over and over. Silvia knew these strange sounds must be the *shaanti's* new password, but she couldn't make them out as a language at all. After almost ten times, she began to get nervous that the snakes would find them before Manuela could manage the strange phrasing. But finally there was silence and in a loud clear tone Manuela spoke the words that would plunge them into the 'heart of darkness:' "Kati ya usiku."

Chapter 16

Into the heart of darkness

EVEN WHEN SHE FELT THE RUSH of warm water and heard the boom of thunder, Manuela kept chanting and squeezing Silvia's hands. In fact, the shock of suddenly 'appearing' in a rainstorm made her squeeze her eyes shut even harder. Only when Silvia yanked her hand away and shouted in her ear did she finally open her eyes.

"Let's get under that tree over there!" Silvia shouted while trying to shield her eyes. The tree was gigantic. Manuela rushed over after Silvia and Fritz. Under the canopy of the dark green, glossy leaves, the water only trickled down, and the girls sat on a gnarly root that had curved outward from the wide swollen trunk of the tree. The air smelled musty and spicy, like old pumpkins rotting in the basement. It also was heavy and hot. Manuela twisted her wet hair up and out of her face and made a knot.

"We really need to think about this riddle. Alfio said we would be safe when we solved it and found the map," said Manuela as she shrugged off her pack and set it beside her. Next to her, Silvia was doing the same and it only took them a few minutes to remember the words together.

"*I am old and drooping too.*" Silvia said. "All I can think of is an old woman's ... *you know,*" she said rolling her eyes.

Manuela smiled. "Well, I hope we don't have to go looking around at *those* to find our map. What could be old that is also in the jungle?" She looked around her as the rain stopped and the animal and insect noises started to sound louder.

"Lot's of animals are probably in here. Probably tigers and crocodiles and ..."

"Cut it out!" Manuela interrupted. "Let's not think about that until we have too." She started and looked over her shoulder as a big red bird with long yellow-tipped wings jumped out of the tree next to them, came chattering to the jungle floor, and then swooped up again.

"O.K. Plants can grow old; maybe an old tree?"

"Yes, but the next line is: *but every year I'm new.* I don't think it's a tree at all." Manuela said. "I think it may be a bird."

"A bird? I wouldn't call a bird 'drooping'," said Silvia as she made a face.

"Its feathers are drooping all over it."

"A bird's feathers don't 'droop,' they ... well, they ... anyway they aren't 'new' every year like a tree's leaves." Silvia said shaking her head.

Manuela just smiled. "Every spring, birds lay 'new' eggs."

"Um ... I don't think they have spring in the rainforest, Manu," Silvia said.

"It's more of a problem for your tree theory then. I don't think rainforest trees shed their leaves for winter here and grow new ones in the spring." Manuela was watching as the red bird dipped between the trees a second time.

"Even pine trees grow pine cones every year at the same time. How else do they get their 'new' trees to grow?" Silvia looked at Manuela smugly.

"Well, the next line is, *Give me the gift that I love most.* Trees don't want anything. But birds want food. So if we find an old bird and give it its favorite food we will get the map." Manuela stood up and grabbed her pack. The rain had stopped and she looked back at Silvia. "Are you coming? We're never going to find anything just sitting here."

After she saw that Silvia was reluctantly following, Manuela started pushing her way through the tall ferns and other big-leafed plants. The raindrops splattered down on her as they rolled off the glossy vegetation. The birds, insects and animals made frightening noises. Steam swirled around in patches as the rain cooled off the hot trees. Neither girl spoke as they trudged along. While keeping an eye out for any particularly old-looking birds, Manuela thought angrily about their conversation. *I don't see why she doesn't agree that it must be a bird! A tree! There must be a zillion trees here. How would we know what tree to pick?* Suddenly she stopped. She heard a loud hissing and, after their recent experience, the sound made her freeze and her skin crawl.

"Why are we stopping? Did you see a bird with a walker?" Silvia said in a teasing voice.

"Shhhh!" Manuela whispered. "I think I just heard a snake hissing."

That was enough for Silvia, who stopped dead in her tracks. Only Fritz didn't seem bothered. He kept sniffing around the ground as if in a frenzy.

Just when Manuela had thought she had heard wrong, a long green and yellow snake dangled down in front of her from a branch above. Manuela felt her skin prickle and her breath start to come in little rasps. The snake ignored her and after slowly spiraling down, dropped the few inches it had left and hurried off into the bush.

Behind her Silvia sighed deeply. Fritz had stopped sniffing and cocked his head to get a look at the snake's tail disappear in the undergrowth. "I don't know if I can keep walking if I might step on one of those." Silvia finally said. Manuela took a deep breath and continued walking.

After about a half an hour of rough going, the girls were soaked to the skin with sweat. The heat and humidity were unbearable, and giant beetles and other strange insects kept popping out of nowhere. Finally, Silvia stopped and refused to go another inch. They had come alongside a steep downhill slope and she pointed out over the canopy of trees visible to their right.

"Look over there. It looks like a river. I don't know about you, but I'm really thirsty and my canteen is empty. Shouldn't we go down there and rest?" Manuela didn't object, and the two easily made it down the ridge to the water.

After refreshing themselves and their canteens, they sat on an old log to eat the cheese sandwiches Alfio had packed for them. As they sat munching, a huge rhinoceros came out from the jungle on the other side of the river and waded in to drink. Its hide was a light grey and it was so close, the girls could see the deep wrinkles and dried mud along its flanks. They could also see its huge horn flashing in the sunlight.

"Don't say anything, Silvi," Manuela whispered. The rhino looked up at them and flicked its ears. When it didn't hear anything else, it put its head back down and got back to its business. Manuela was practically holding her breath until she saw the huge creature lumber back off the way it came.

"Boy, do I wish I had a camera," Silvia said softly. "I hope we get to see other animals close up like that before we find that ancient tree."

Manuela shook her head. "I hope we *don't*. Don't you get how much danger we are in? This is all some silly game to you." She was still shaking from fear at the thought of that horn. "And for the last time, we aren't looking for a *tree*, we are looking for a ..." Manuela didn't get to finish her sentence because a group of small chimpanzees jumped down into the water from some branches above. They were so close, water splashed on Fritz, who backed up and hid behind Silvia's legs.

"What ..." Silvia stuttered. The chimps were splashing and screeching. Then they turned to the girls and gave ferocious smiles, showing their ugly yellow teeth. "Let's get out of here," she said as she grabbed her backpack and started scrambling up the hill.

Manuela was right behind her. As she grabbed at roots and vines, she looked over her shoulder and was shocked to see that the chimps were following them! After much struggling, they managed to make it back up to the top of the ridge. They tried to run as fast as they could but they couldn't go very fast with all the vegetation. Fritz kept turning around and barking while the chimps screeched a sort of laugh and threw seedpods and other things down on him.

Then Silvia slipped and they had to stop. Her left foot was stuck in some kind of red mud.

"Help me out!" she yelled at Manuela while the monkeys cackled overhead. Manuela tugged and tugged and, finally, she was able to get Silvia's leg free. But not the shoe. When Silvia finally got the shoe to come loose, it came out with a loud squelching sound that set the chimps tittering loudly. But throughout the whole ordeal, not one chimp came down or tried to hurt or even touch them.

Manuela looked herself and Silvia over. Not just their feet, but every inch of their bodies was covered in mud. They had red mud on their feet and legs, black mud on their bodies and arms, and a light brown mud all over their faces and hair. *We almost could pass for natives,* thought Manuela.

"Well, I guess we better get used to having company. It doesn't look like they are going to leave us alone," Manuela said. Silvia agreed and they started off again.

"I still don't see how we are going to know when we find what we are looking for." Silvia was sweating, but the sun was not overhead anymore.

"I'm sure we'll know when we need to," Manuela answered.

"Oh, that makes me feel so much better." Silvia said. She had found a branch and was now using it like a staff, hacking occasionally at the thick plants underfoot.

"Why do you think I know? You don't even believe my answer to the riddle."

"But your answer is wrong!" Silvia yelled back.

Manuela was frustrated, but she didn't have time to answer back. Silvia stabbed her stick into the ground in front of her and immediately — WHOOSH!

The two girls and their dog found themselves hanging with their feet over their head nestled in a net about eight feet off the ground.

Chapter 17

Silvia puts her hand in animal poop

FRITZ KEPT WHINING and wriggling which pushed Silvia's face deeper into the net. She was so surprised when it first happened; she had thought some giant bird had come to pluck her out of the sky. Now, about ten minutes had passed, and she could feel the blood rushing to her head and Fritz's shoulder blades pressing into her back.

"There has to be a way out. Maybe if we swayed back and forth, the net will fall away from whatever it's tied to," Manuela said.

"We've *been* swaying back and forth. Besides, I think whoever made this net probably thought of that." Silvia wriggled her nose as a fly tried to settle there. The smell of the drying mud was really terrible and she was trying to breathe only through her mouth.

"I don't know if I want to meet whoever made this net," Manuela said a few minutes later.

But off in the distance the girls could hear strange chanting and drums, and they knew that their captors were on their way. Sure enough, as the chanting got louder, gaudily painted men stepped out to circle them. Silvia wasn't too sure, being upside down, but they seemed ... little. They were ferocious looking, however. With white and red paint slashes all over their bare bodies and huge feathers and bones sticking out, the natives looked like human birds.

No one said anything. Fritz had even stopped wriggling. Then one of the little men, the one with the largest collection of feathers and bones on him, came forward and said something to them in some very strange language. Silvia thought it best to answer even though she doubted they would understand. But on this trip, one couldn't be sure about anything.

"We don't know what you are saying or what you want, but we definitely don't want to bother you," she said as best she could with her mouth squashed up against the net.

"Please, don't hurt us. We're sorry if we did anything wrong." Manuela sounded almost desperate. Little Blue Feather only looked confused and said something like "Tafadhali njoo na mimi! Ni muhimu sana." Then he motioned to his men, and they came closer and stuck spears up to the net.

"They're going to kill us!" Manuela screamed. Silvia just held her breath and closed her eyes. All of a sudden they felt the spears tugging and they toppled to the ground. Apart from some bruises and scratches, they seemed to be alright. Then the men pointed the spears at them and they understood perfectly well that they wanted the girls to follow Little Blue Feather into the brush.

Whenever one of them so much as coughed or sniffed, they felt the butt end of a spear in their side, so the walk to the little natives' village was quiet except for the crunch of vegetation underneath. Silvia's nose was frustratingly itchy, but the short tribesmen had tied the girls' hands behind their backs and there was nothing she could do. Worse than the itch was the thought that maybe these were Rogs and they were doomed.

Soon enough a small clearing came suddenly into view. It had thatched huts just like on T.V., and lots of naked people came running over to see them. These people weren't as scary because they had only occasional splotches of yellow paint on their stomachs or arms. Some had bones through their noses. One really small woman had a huge disc in her lip which pulled it down to her chin. The women all carried babies. Silvia, Fritz and Manuela were put in a thatch hut with two guards outside the door.

"Do you think they are going to eat us?" asked Silvia quietly. She had heard that cannibals might still be around.

"I really don't know, but I don't think so. They didn't try to hurt us, and they looked like they were expecting someone else. If they wanted to eat us, they would have killed us right away, I think," Manuela said. "But I can't think they have anything good in mind for us."

Silvia took the cedro out of her pack and smelled its faint citrus aroma.

"You should put that back. What if they take it?"

Silvia rolled her eyes. "They can take it from my pack any time they want anyway. Besides, I thought we might be able to use it to understand what they are saying."

"But these aren't Rogs. Alfio said it would help us with the *Rogs'* language." Manuela reached out for the fruit.

Silvia pulled it away. "How do you know they aren't Rogs? They sure don't look normal to me."

"The *other* Rogs spoke to us in English, that's how. Now put it away!" Manuela tried to get the fruit out of her hands, but Silvia snapped her arms back. She snapped them so quickly that she lost hold of the cedro and it rolled through the loose grass at the back of the hut.

"Oh, great!" Manuela said angrily. They crouched down and tried to peek through the straw. The cedro was lying about a foot away next to a pile of animal dung.

"Now look what you've done. How are we going to get it now?"

Silvia clenched her jaw and went to sit on the other side of the hut. *It's always my fault! No matter what happens,* she thought. *Things will never change.*

Just then, a little man a little fatter than those who brought them to the village pushed away the straw doorway and bent to come into the hut. He carried some bowls of what looked like stew and mash. He sat them down in the middle of the hut, and with a goofy grin, made eating motions with his hands and then left. Silvia couldn't resist. Her stomach had been grumbling and the stew smelled like her uncle's lamb stew. She scooted to the bowls and began trying to eat the mash and stew with her fingers. It wasn't bad at all. She looked up to see Manuela staring at her with hard eyes.

"Well, it's either starve or eat it. If it is poison, then we aren't any worse off," she said between mouthfuls.

Manuela didn't say anything but just looked away. Silvia felt her heart flutter. She really was sorry about the cedro. *But if she just would've let me look at it and say what I had to say!*

After half the food was gone, Silvia pushed the bowls aside and went back to the other side of the hut. She felt better for the warm food, but Manuela was still angry so she felt miserable. *We've got to get out of here fast and get that cedro. I know I'm right about the tree this time.* Silvia hugged her legs together and closed her eyes.

"Silvia, wake up!" Manuela said urgently but quietly. Silvia realized that she was being shaken and groggily opened her eyes. It was dark, and she could just barely make out Manuela in the patchy light that filtered in through the grass walls of the hut.

"Silvi, they sound like they are getting ready to do something out there," Manuela said still shaking her sister.

"O.K, O.K., you can stop shaking me now." Silvia rubbed her eyes and stretched her kinked back. "What's that weird music?"

"That's what I've been trying to tell you. If you peek out through the grass there," Manuela pointed to a chink which let some light in, "you can see them all dressed up and singing and drumming by a big fire."

Silvia slid over to the wall and looked out. At first she could only see the backside of one of the guards, but then he sat down again next to their door, and the spectacle she saw made her bite her bottom lip. A tall bonfire was raging in the center of the clearing despite the heat and humidity. All along one side the small tribesmen were lined up covered in feathers, paint and animal hide loin cloths. The women had purple and white markings on their faces and breasts, and their hair was sticking out in outrageous star patterns. The air had a burnt hair smell, and the pounding of the drums and moans of the people made Silvia's stomach knot up.

"We have to get out of here right away." Silvia backed away from the hole. She noticed Fritz was pacing back and forth near the back of the hut and sniffing at the bottom of the wall there. "What is it boy? Are you still trying to get the cedro?"

"Actually, I think he has to go the bathroom. I know I do. I guess these people think we'll dig a hole in the corner or something." Manuela said.

As the girls sat trying to think of a way out, Fritz started pulling on the grass wall in the back of the hut with his teeth. Silvia looked over in time to see him squirm his way through the tiny hole and disappear.

"Fritz! What are you doing!" yelled Manuela under her breath. The girls were at the hole in a second but it was too late. They saw Fritz disappear behind a tree in the dark. The cedro was still there, barely visible in the shadow's hut. But the hole was too small for them to fit through.

The girls held their breath as they waited to see if any of the natives had noticed the breakout. But the chanting of the warriors and the crackling of the bonfire covered up any other sounds. Manuela looked at Silvia and raised her eyebrows. Silvia shrugged and bent down to try to rip off more grass. It was hard but they managed to unweave enough to squeeze through.

Silvia went first, pushing her pack out in front. The stench was horrendous and she had to stop herself from retching. As soon as she was all the way out, she grabbed the cedro and stuffed it in her dirty pack. Immediately she realized she had grabbed something else too and she repulsively tried to wipe off the dung on some big leafy plant.

"Come on! Help me out!" Manuela called from behind her.

156

"Just a minute. I stuck my hand in that animal poop."

"Forget it. I can pull myself out." Silvia heard a scraping sound behind her, and then Manuela was standing beside her. "Yuck. You smell as bad as you look."

"Well, you smell but look worse." Silvia put on her pack and quietly the girls picked their way into the dark.

Chapter 18

The girls find the answer to the riddle

AFTER A FEW MINUTES OF NERVOUSNESS, they realized the tribesmen weren't looking for them, but they still hadn't found Fritz. Also, it wouldn't be long before the warriors *would* be after them, not to mention other predators. They had brought out their flashlights, which helped them, but they could be seen easily.

"Maybe we should find a tree and climb it," Manuela suggested.

"So we can sit and wait for them to come right to us? Our feet are leaving huge footprints in this icky mud we've been walking through." Silvia shined her light on the ground by their feet.

"Well, what then." Manuela asked hotly. "I'm tired and hungry and —"

"Well, if you would have eaten that stew, you would only be tired."

"I'm surprised you didn't eat it all yourself," Manuela said. She shined her light ahead of them, but all they could see were more trees, vines and eyes.

"Fritz will find us. I'm sure he will." Silvia was just about to continue walking when she heard a bark coming from their far left.

"That's got to be Fritz!" she said and started in that direction. Manuela was close behind. After about ten seconds, Silvia stopped.

"Ow," Manuela said, bumping into her. "What are you doing?"

"I don't hear him. I don't know which way to go."

"There. Listen." Manuela put her hand on Silvia's shoulder. Sure enough, a faint barking was coming from way ahead. The girls kept going even though it was slow moving. In the dark, with one hand on a flashlight, it was hard to see through all the undergrowth. Every so often, they could hear a bark, and the barks sounded closer every time.

As they approached the barking sound, they also heard a loud sound of water rushing. When they finally stepped out onto a cleared ledge, they could see they were above a river and waterfall. Fritz came bounding over to them and nuzzled each in turn.

There was light in the clearing, coming from an enormous full pink moon low overhead. The water seemed to sparkle like a rippled rainbow. Even through their caked-on smell, they could smell the sweet, heavy flowers when they took deep breaths. About twenty yards away, a big tree stretched out towards the sky and river. Nothing else was around except a large group of strange animals that looked like half donkeys, half zebras. Their face and bodies were brown, but their legs and bottoms were white with black stripes like a zebra.

"Well, Fritz. Who are your friends?" Manuela asked smiling.

The strange animals slowly walked away from the tree and into the tall grass as the girls approached with Fritz. But they stayed there, peering out from between the blades.

It was the biggest tree Silvia had ever seen. The trunk was easily as wide as a swimming pool. And the bumps and knots! It seemed as if its bark had been boiled and it dried in that crusty, blistered condition. A dusty pale brown, it was streaked with red sap. Drooping from the branches were myriads of giant, glossy, dark moss-colored leaves and big pearl-colored crinkly flowers with purple puffs. The air surrounding the tree was sweet like a cantaloupe.

Silvia ran her hands along the rough bark. *This has to be the old and drooping thing,* she thought. *I have to find a way to prove it to Manu.* Slowly she walked to her right, running her hand along the tree trunk as she went. Occasionally, she stopped and reached up to feel a smooth glossy leaf and to trace its pale green center vein with her finger or inhale the sweet melon fragrance of the creamy flowers.

It took them a few minutes to get all around the tree. When they had almost come full circle, she found it. Part of the tree was engraved. The lettering was strange, almost like wrinkles randomly thrown together, but Silvia was sure that she had found some sort of inscription.

"Look here, Manu. What do you think of this?" Silvia watched carefully as Manuela felt the inscription with her hand.

"It does look old and drooping, Silvia," Manuela said without sarcasm. "But what could this possibly be?"

"*I am old and drooping too, but every year I'm new; give me the gift that I love most, and I will give to you.* Maybe the flowers are what are new every year. But what could be the gift that it loves the most?" Silvia sat down and stared

161

up at the strange carvings. When she put her pack beside her, Fritz began nosing around the opening.

"Sorry, Fritz, I don't have anything for you to eat. You and Manu are going to have to find some berries or something." Silvia pushed Fritz's nose away. When she did, the cedru fell out and Fritz tried to grab it with his teeth.

"Hey! Don't do that!" Silvia yelled as she tried to grab it from under his nose.

"Fritz, you can't eat that!" Manuela shouted, tackling the dog. The cedru bounced away and Silvia reached out and grabbed it.

"I wish this cedru would stop being such a trouble and actually *help* us," Silvia said, shoving it back in her pack.

"Wait a minute! I just had an idea," Manuela said. "What if those markings are *Rog* script? Maybe the juice from the cedru will unlock their meaning?"

Silvia pulled the citrus fruit back out of her pack and looked at it skeptically. "Alfio said if we drank the juice it would help us understand the Rog language."

"No. He said we could *use* the juice to understand the Rog language," Manuela said excitedly as she grabbed the cedru.

"I guess it can't hurt to try to rub a little on the tree. But we shouldn't use it all," Silvia said.

Manuela picked at the lemony peel until she had a patch peeled the size of a quarter. Then she stuck her finger in to puncture the juicy segments. The sweet lemon scent sprayed out and tickled their noses. Slowly, Manuela brought the fruit up to the inscription and began rubbing juice across the strange wrinkles.

Silvia didn't know if it was the cedru's juice that sprayed into her eye, but her vision began to blur as she tried to focus it on the tree. She blinked a few times and opened her eyes wide and looked at the inscription again. It read:

I am old and drooping too,
But every year I'm new;
Give me the gift that I love most,
And I will give to you.

"Do you see what I see?" asked Manuela with a whisper. "I think you may have been right about the tree theory."

"Now what?" Silvia said not daring to move her eyes away from the strange transformed inscription. "If that cedru juice is what this tree loves the most, what to we get?"

As if in answer to her question, the girls saw a huge orange butterfly come flying straight out of the tree, not three feet up to the right. When Fritz went over to investigate, they could see that there was really a hole there, an entranceway into the tree trunk that wasn't there before. Glancing at each other, the sisters knew that they had to go in if they were ever going to get the *Tala Pahaad.*

"You go first," Manuela said, putting the cedru in her backpack.

"I think Fritz should go first. He can tell if anything is wrong right away."

"O.K." Manuela said quickly. "I mean *after* Fritz. You were the one who thought it was a tree."

"Oh, thanks. Maybe you're just afraid that …" But Fritz had jumped into the tunnel and Manuela pushed Silvia to follow, so she shouldered her pack and climbed up the pale knotty tree bark to the hole. Looking in, she didn't see anything but blackness and her heart skipped a little as she remembered Bolivia just days before.

"Come on, Silvi. Get going before those painted pyg-mies find us here."

Taking a deep breath, Silvia bent forward and crawled into the dark.

Chapter 19

The magic library

THE TUNNEL WAS ROUGH and very hot. Once Manuela thought she wasn't going to make it through it narrowed so much. But she backed up and took off her backpack and pushed it on ahead of her and was able to pass. She felt something crawling on her leg and screamed.

"Can't you go any faster, Silvi! I can't stand this!" Manuela pushed her backpack against Silvia's shoes.

"Hold on! I can see light up there around a turn," Silvia yelled back. After a few more horrible minutes, Manuela was climbing out of the hole into a circular room carved out of the middle of the tree. Way up above, she could see sunlight coming through waving green leaves.

As she inhaled, Manuela realized it wasn't as hot or humid here. But that wasn't the oddest thing. It was a library. All along the circular wall were shelves carved into the wood of the tree, and they were filled with old, ancient-looking books. The floor was smooth pale wood, and in the center a group of stone structures covered in moss rose up around a flat stone 'table.'

Silvia was already walking around the perimeter looking at the dusty books. "This is incredible," she said. "In the middle of a tree, in the middle of the *jungle*." She pulled out one large book bound in red leather with the title *Gates and Their Keepers*.

"This book must be a thousand years old! Just look at the crinkly pages."

The sky grew dim and the light inside the 'library' waned for a moment and then came back. "I think we had better find that book of the mountain fast. Who knows how or when we will have to leave?" Manuela said.

Silvia put the book back, and the two of them started slowly walking around the room looking at the shelves. Fritz curled up on one of the stone 'couches' and took a nap. It was difficult to read the titles of all the books; some weren't on the spine, and many were written in strange script. Manuela hoped that it wouldn't be so obscure that they would have to go through all the books.

"Kule."

Silvia looked over at Manuela. "What did you say?"

"I didn't say anything."

"Yes you did." Silvia turned back to the bookshelves.

"Kule," said a hushed voice. Silvia spinned around. "O.K. That's enough fooling around, Manu."

Manuela looked angry. "But I told you, I didn't say …"

"Kule!" The voice was a little louder this time. A small woman with the same black skin and hair as the warriors came out of the shadows. She wore a pale tan cloth wrapped around her body and had many strands of bones heaped around her neck. Her eyes were wide and deeply set. When she came closer, they could see huge red discs pulling her earlobes down to her shoulders.

"It's a trap," Manuela said softly.

"No, no trap," the woman whispered smiling. "Kule, over there." She pointed to the other end of the tree. The girls didn't move. "What wrong?" the woman asked frowning. "I say 'over there'. You want map-book, no?"

Silvia was sure this must be a contact. "Yes! Are you a contact from the DragonFlies?"

Manuela glared at her.

"I Mti Mwanamke, 'Tree-Woman'. Hurry. Not much time."

"Time for what?" Silvia asked?

"They come. The others. The deep-Baku in war with them. They smell you."

Manuela looked down at herself. "I smell me." The tiny woman made a motion with her hand to hurry the girls over. Silvia followed, but Manuela stayed back.

After a minute, Silvia called Manuela over. "I found some books with the word *Tala* in it. Maybe it *is* on this shelf." When Manuela walked over, Silvia pointed to a row on the bottom shelf with books of all colors and sizes.

"Alright. You start at that end and I'll start over here," Manuela said bending down to check out the titles: *Samaya, Janataa, Buddhi*. The old woman just kept nodding her tightly wound mound of graying hair. Finally, Manuela pulled out a tall but very thin book with a greasy black leather cover. On the front, written in a glowing red were the words *Tala Pahaad*.

"I've got it!" she yelled, as she straightened up. "Let's take it over to the stone table." Manuela carried the light-weight book with care and placed it on top of the low table. The girls held their breath as Manuela opened the front cover. It creaked open to show a blank page. Quickly, Silvia turned the page. It, too, was blank. Manuela began to panic as she turned page after page to discover them all blank.

"This isn't good at all," Silvia said as Manuela turned the last page to uncover the back cover. "What good is a blank book going to do us?" They both looked up at the pygmy woman. Mti was just softly smiling at them. Then she winked.

"Maybe it isn't blank," said Manuela quietly.

"What do you mean? You can see for yourself."

"But we used the cedro on the inscription to under-stand that. Maybe the cedro juice will uncover the maps in this book." Manuela brought out the fruit and looked up at Silvia. When Silvia nodded, Manuela squeezed a tiny drop onto the last page and wiped it into a streak with her finger. Nothing happened. Time seemed to stand still as Manuela inhaled the fresh citrus and the dark mustiness of the room. She could hear the trees swaying overhead as if a storm were brewing and saw that the room had become quite shadowy. Then suddenly the streak became black patches.

"This big lemon is sure becoming very useful. No wonder Alfio said to use it carefully," Silvia said softly.

Overhead they heard a crack of thunder and a streak of lightening lit up the room. Fritz leaped to his feet and growled into the blackness that followed.

"What is it, Fritz?" Silvia said placing her hand on his collar. "Manu, his hair is standing on end!"

"We've got to get out of here fast. I bet the warriors have tracked us here," Manuela said, gathering the book and the cedru and putting them in her pack.

"Or the Rogs. Or both." Silvia shivered. "Is it me, or is it cold in here now?"

"No, no. Not pygmy. They want to protect you in hut. You run. The others smell you. It is others."

Another crack of lightening lit up the room and this time both girls saw what Fritz was growling at. Coming out of the hole that led into the room, and standing on either side of it, were warriors. But they weren't small. Their long thin limbs seemed like skeleton bones, and their white painted faces glowed as an afterimage when the lightening was gone.

Apart from the wind and rumbling overhead, there wasn't a sound. Manuela grabbed Silvia's hand and slowly backed down and around one of the stone seats to shield them from the warriors. Fritz came as Silvia pulled him, snarling under his breath.

"We know you are there. Come out now," a low clear voice said. Manuela was surprised to hear the plain American English. It couldn't be one of the warriors.

"Manu," whispered Silvia, "there's a hole in that table."

"What?"

"Look at the stone table. Where the book was is now a shimmering hole. And Mti is gone. I don't see her anywhere." Silvia said calmly. Manuela could barely see the table in the dark, but the shimmering hole was definitely there. It was like it was covered in cobwebs.

"It's the only way out, Manu. We have to try to get in there."

"Those warriors are just going to go in after us. What if it's a dead end?" Manuela shivered at the thought.

"Fanya haraka! I say COME OUT!" the voice demanded.

"It is over." Just then a loud crack practically shook Manuela out of her skin and she could see a tall, fat shriveled raisin-colored *thing* blocking the view of the hole and the warriors. Its body was round and covered in patches of bristly black hair. Long black hair was combed straight up from its head and stood frozen like that. Instead of arms, four silver snakes were slithering out from its belly and flicking out fire-red tongues at the girls. But by far the worst image that they were left with when the lightning faded was its four pale eyes with fuchsia slits staring right at them.

Fritz whimpered beside them and they heard scuttling. Without loosing a second, they grabbed hands and Silvia held on to Fritz.

"We don't have a choice. There's no time to argue. Now!" Silvia screamed as Manuela felt Silvia squeezing her hand. They stood up and jumped onto the table, which was now just a big hole covered in a strange mist.

All of a sudden the floor dropped out from beneath them and they were sliding. Manuela opened her eyes to see the world traveling away from her and disappearing into a tiny pinpoint of light above them. Holding on tightly to Silvia, she bumped her way down into the cold, slimy pit which had opened up. Above them, far away, a loud fiendish howl seemed to cut off prematurely.

Chapter 20

Journey to the
center of the earth

THE STRANGE FALL SEEMED to last forever, yet they didn't seem to be falling very fast, or toppling over at all. All around them a faint grey bubble shimmered and made it seem as if they were on a new type of roller coaster.

All at once, they slowed and the bubble popped. The staleness of the air hit Manuela and the damp coolness of it made her skin crawl. She could hear loud dripping noises everywhere. When Fritz barked, the echo that came back in the darkness went on for so long that Manuela thought it sounded as if there were a pack of dogs all around them. Then Silvia turned on her flashlight and illuminated the stalagmites and stalactites around them.

"We're in a cave," Silvia said as she flashed her light around the space. "This place is really big; it's at least three floors high, don't you think?"

"It's beautiful. Look at the way the wall has all these snowflake-like crystals." Manuela shined her own flashlight on them and watched them change from pink to blue to yellow. Then she shined her light all along the wall until she saw that the cave had a doorway other than the one overhead from which they entered.

"Look at that, Silvi." Manuela walked over to the tunnel and shined her light in. The light dimmed into nothing along the walkway that was just about the right height for a hallway in any building. In the quiet dripping, Manuela could make out faint beating sounds, almost like drums.

"Manu, do you hear that music?" Silvia asked shining her light on her sister. Manuela winced at the light in her eyes and Silvia lowered the light.

"Do you think it's music?" she asked as she tried to listen to the faint sounds.

"Well, it sounds like drums to me. Let's go and see what it is. We can't stay here, anyway." Silvia said starting off down the corridor.

"Wait!" Manuela called after her. "Let's finish looking at the maps we found. Maybe they will tell us where we are."

Silvia came back and shined her light on Manuela as she pulled out the thin book and the cedru. Soon the curled pages were filled with black ink markings which looked like mazes. Most of them looked like snowflakes. The one on the last page was the largest and most decorated. In the center of the snowflake was a big space filled with a terrible looking face with four eyes and monstrous teeth.

"I bet this one is where the Rogs are. I don't think I could ever forget those four eyes," Silvia said with a shudder.

"But how are we to know where we are now? And what kind of map is a snowflake maze? This isn't going to help us at all!" Manuela put what remained of the cedru back in her pack and carefully closed the *Tala Pahaad*. After shaking her head, she put it in her pack too.

"Well, there's only one way to go from here so we might as well get started," Silvia said, shining her light down the corridor and setting off again.

Manuela hesitated only a moment. After shining her light back at the hole in the ceiling of the cavern, she hurried after Silvia and Fritz.

The girls walked in silence except for their footsteps which echoed in the limestone tunnel. As they walked along, the walls and ceiling had begun to glow of their own accord from a strange bright yellow moss that clung like peach fuzz to the slimy walls. Ducking between stalactites and stepping around stalagmites that occasionally blocked the way, Manuela wondered at Silvia's silence.

"Are you alright, Silvi?" she asked in a whisper. Every sound seemed so loud.

"Do you think it's a trap?" Silvia asked after a short pause. "Do you think that … silver thing … is behind us?"

So that's it, thought Manuela. *She's afraid.* "If it is, I don't think it's very close. We'd hear *anything* in these caves."

The girls had put their flashlights back in their packs a while ago to save them since the fluorescent moss was enough to travel by. Now in the dim light Silvia stopped and pointed ahead of her. "I just feel like this is no accident. Look. Those look like stairs. Who could have made stairs in a place like this?"

Manuela could see where the tunnel began sloping downwards and that steps had been carved out of the limestone. The yellow-gold lichen covered them except for what looked like a worn path down the middle. The music, for they could tell it was music by now, had been getting louder and now they could hear strange voices as well.

"At least we are going *somewhere*. I think I'd feel more afraid if there weren't any stairs or music. Then what would we do?" Manuela hesitated beside Silvia. Even in the darkness, she could see the dried mud all over her crumbling and crusting her hair. She looked tired and hungry and afraid. *What if we can't find Jiwan? Or what if we find him, but are unable to free him? What will happen to us then?* Fighting the impulse to cry, Manuela reached out and grabbed her sister's hand and squeezed it. Together, they started down the spiraling stairs.

The stairs were slippery, and twice Manuela slipped and almost fell. Fritz took his time gingerly stepping down the stairs sideways. As they descended, the air grew cooler and damper. Finally, as they came around a final bend, she could see the tunnel open out into a larger area that glowed with dancing light. Drums were beating and voices chanted in time with strange grunts and howls.

As they emerged from the tunnel, enormous stalagmites rose up on their right and blocked their view. The cavern's wall, on their left, was as least 300 feet high and illuminated with dancing shadows and fiery orange light coming from the center of the giant hall.

Sneaking up behind a broken stalagmite, Manuela and Silvia peeked out at the scene beyond and below. They were on a ledge, and some 15 feet down, the cavern floor began and spread out in a huge circumference as big as a football field. At the center of the stone floor, a giant bonfire was crackling and leaping. Smoke plumes rose up and spiraled out tunnels in the ceiling. The light from the fire enabled them to see what was making the drumming and chanting.

In a giant circle, disgusting black beetle-bodied things about three feet high were jumping up and down on stubby red feet. Stumpy tails stuck out behind them and they had their four red arms flung out and waving. Resisting the urge to vomit, Manuela saw that they were covered in oozing green mucus, and that in their open mouths, their teeth were actually wiggling.

On a giant stone column painted white and black, one of the Rogs (it was obvious that was what they were seeing) who was a little bigger and fatter, and covered with bigger black bumps oozing mucus, stood with its hands to its sides. Suddenly it raised its four arms and the drumming stopped as the Rogs all stopped jumping and chanting in unison.

"Urrrtt shshshsintig. Urrrtt wheghtin yuk ..." began the Rog on the pedestal.

"Quick! The cedru!" Silvia whispered. Manuela pulled out the fruit, and the two sipped the last of the juice. Immediately, the Rog captain's words began to sound different.

"... We will make them weep! Our storm will make them burn! I, huri, will lead us to freedom! ..."

"Do you think that is Shatru's army?" Silvia asked.

"Shhh! Let's listen while we can."

"After the fall of jiwan, we will be able to take kingdoms above. The people will feel the blackness and despair that they long for. Their only hope will be their pain!" The Rogs let out a cheer and began stamping. Huri put up two of his arms and they fell silent again.

175

"Our victory is almost upon us, but we need to fight still again. Dushta here has said that his scouts have spotted Hira and her DragonFly bugs on their way." Huri stopped as the Rogs rumbled displeasure and rage. "This time we must take Hira herself. Shatru has ordered that she be brought to the place of the Time of the End so that Jiwan will give up his power. REMEMBER!" Huri bellowed, "Hira must be taken alive!" The Rogs howled in displeasure. "BUT THE DRAGONFLY BUGS CAN BE MASSACRED!" Huri raised all of his red oozy arms above him and opened his mouth wide. His teeth wiggled creepily as he let out a loud wailing noise, which caused the other Rogs to begin wailing as well.

Manuela had to cover her ears because the echo of the wails was so loud. Fritz had buried his head in between the two girls as they crouched behind the massive stalagmite. As the wails turned back to more drumming and chanting, Manuela turned to Silvia and uncovered her sister's ears.

"Did you hear that? Hira is coming! She'll know what to do to save her father!" Manuela said excitedly. Silvia was about to answer when a loud roar went up from the Rog troops, accompanied by a buzzing noise.

They looked back out into the fiery cavern to see a hazy blue cloud come ripping down a tunnel across the cave near the ceiling. The cloud roared in a swift circle around the Rogs and then froze in mid-air as hundreds of DragonFly people materialized. Manuela had been expecting to see more of the little fairy-like creatures that had visited her in Aru's hut. But these creatures were as tall as she was and had long lean bluish silver bodies with four golden-tipped purple wings. Their hair was like braided gauze as it sprung out around their narrow faces in blue-sparking puffs.

"HIRA! Show yourself so that the battle may begin!" Huri growled amid the commotion. DragonFly soldiers with acid violet eyes stared down at the ugly monsters below them.

Even the Rogs grew quiet when they saw the slightly smaller luminescent silver Hira rise out from the ring of blue soldiers. Huge gossamer wings of pale cerulean and tangerine spread out behind her, and her hair spun up like pale pink cotton candy into tiny wisps. What seemed to transfix Manuela the most was the Dragonfly Keeper's daughter's dress. Like a wave of light, thousands upon thousands of tiny iridescent threads so thin were woven into a very short-fronted skirt with a train so long that it floated three feet behind her. It sparkled in a way that made it seem of no color, only light.

"Huri. Captian of the Demon-King. We have come to reclaim my father, Jiwan, Keeper of the Dragonfly Magic." Hira said with a hushed high whisper of a voice.

"Ha!" Huri smirked. "You don't even know where we are keeping him! How can you claim to have the power to reclaim him?"

"Huri, we do not like bloodshed, even of the Rog kind. However, we will do what it takes to bring Jiwan back to his garden." Hira's voice floated out into the cavern and echoed like tiny pebbles thrown in an empty well.

"YOU CANNOT HAVE HIM!" bellowed Huri. The Rogs followed with a roar of their own. "Hira, daughter of Jiwan. Prepare for the Time of the End!" Huri screamed and the Rogs began shooting what looked like black darts up into the ring of DragonFly soldiers.

Chapter 21

Saving Hira

ILVIA AND MANUELA DUCKED back down against the stalagmite out of sight. In the instant before they had ducked, Manuela had seen some of the dark darts explode with needles into the thin wings of the DragonFly soldiers. They had opened their violet eyes wide in agony and then spiraled into the mass of waiting monsters below.

During the battle, the girls huddled together and cringed at every ethereal scream and blood-curdling growl. Fritz stayed down between them, and Manuela could feel him shivering. They could hear strange buzzing, bleating, and horrible wet gurgling sounds. The shadows of the warriors flicked across the back wall they faced and the smell of singed hair and burnt flesh stung their noses as the bonfire crackled and consumed the victims of the fight. Manuela clung to Silvia and Fritz and realized how much they depended on each other. If they could trust each other, really trust each other, then maybe they had a chance to survive.

Suddenly a roar of victory went up from the Rogs and the buzzing stopped. The girls turned around slowly and peered through the limestone shadows to see Hira enclosed in a fiery red mesh globe. It hung suspended from an extension of the ledge they were on but about 200 feet further ahead across the room. She sat slumped and folded, her gossamer wings drooping and smoky. But she was alive. The rest of the hundreds of DragonFly soldiers lay in blue and purple heaps underneath the red slimy feet of the Rogs.

"Hira, you can now see your father, Jiwan. But not to reclaim him. You will join him in eternal emptiness after we suck him dry of his Magic." Huri yelled across at the captured DragonFly Daughter. He had lost two arms in the battle and they were dripping foamy grey spittle down his body. At least half of the Rogs had fallen as well, covering the ground in their black turtle-like shells. The surviving Rogs walked all over them as if they were blown-out tires.

Hira didn't answer. Her head was bowed and her pinkish hair was curling and waving in an unseen breeze. She had her slender silver arms wrapped around her knees and the faint glow of her fantastic dress dripped out between the red mesh of the globe.

"We've got to try to get to her. If we can't save her, then Jiwan and the DragonFly Kingdom are going to be hard to save," Silvia whispered.

"I think we can sneak around the ledge behind these stalagmites, but how are we going to get her out of that red globe?" Manuela sighed. "We don't even know what it's made of."

"Let's just get over there first. Maybe we'll think of something on the way," Silvia said as she started to walk crouched-over in the direction of the globe.

Fritz followed behind Manuela, close to her heels. The stench in the cave-hall was horrible after the battle, and the bonfire had heated the room to an almost unbearable degree. Manuela kept brushing the dirty sweat out of her eyes and hoped she wouldn't faint from dehydration.

While they were making their way towards Hira's globe, Huri and his Rogs were assessing their damage and taking care of their wounds. Every so often, Silvia and Manuela would peek between the stalagmites to check their progress and the state of things below.

Finally, they were directly behind the extension that held Hira's globe. It was only about five feet long and seemed to be carved right out of the limestone. Manuela guessed that it was wide enough to walk on. *But how are we going to get her out of there, and what do we do then?* Just then she had an idea.

"Silvia! The river pearl that Sir Luta gave us. I still have it."

"Of course! He said it would take us somewhere safe. But how do we get to Hira?" Silvia peeked out at the Rogs below. Manuela had noticed that they seemed to be busy packing things.

"If we can just get her to reach up and hold on to one of us, then we should be able to take her with us when we use the pearl," Manuela said as she pulled out the tiny steel-gray jewel. "Fritz, you stay close to us when we get out there. We'll only have a minute to spare and we need to be together when I count to three."

Manuela and Silvia tightened their packs and took deep breaths. When Manuela thought they were ready she nodded to Silvia. "You go first and get Hira's attention. Get her to reach up and grab your hand as soon as possible.

When she does, yell "Now," and then count to three and think of a safe place.

"Is that how it works? What if you think of a different place than me?" Silvia asked

"Don't argue now! Just think about feeling safe. I'm sure if it were more complicated than that, Sir Luta would have mentioned it."

Silvia looked worried but didn't say anything. She took a deep breath and slowly inched her way to the stalagmite opening that led out onto the extension. She knew they had to be fast. *What if she doesn't grab hold of my hand? What if the pearl doesn't work like we think?* Silvia was trembling with fear as she tried not to gag from the stink of the carnage below.

When she felt a tap from behind, Silvia knew that it was time. Swallowing hard, she shot out towards the hanging globe, making sure not to slip on the slimy limestone. In a second she was at the globe bending down and looking into the silvery-grey eyes of Hira, who raised her head startled to gaze in wonder at the two girls and the dog.

"Hira, we're here to get you out. Do you understand? We don't have any time. Just grab hold of my hand!" Silvia whispered. She thrust out her hand and luckily it went through the strange glowing fiber that made up the globe. Hira's look of despair vanished and she nodded, her large bold eyes shining in the cavern shadows.

When Silvia felt Hira grab hold of her hand, she squeezed Manuela's hand as a signal. She closed her eyes and waited. Manuela's voice sounded hoarse behind her. "One. Two. Thr …"

"WHAT IS THAT?! DUSHTA — KILL THEM!" Huri's awful voice sounded as if he were right there in front of them. Suddenly Silvia heard barking.

"Fritz! No!" Manuela screamed. But suddenly it was silent and Silvia opened her eyes to find she was swirling in a pearl-white cloud that burned her eyes. Immediately she closed them again and held onto the two hands as tightly as possible, feeling as if she were falling through warm bath water.

Chapter 22

Really meeting the DragonFlies

SILVIA SAT UP COUGHING. She felt like her lungs were on fire. When she finally was able to breathe, she noticed that Manuela had her arms around her and was offering her some cool water from her canteen. Silvia grabbed it and drank it down gratefully.

"I think it's the smoke," Manuela said, taking the canteen back from Silvia. "I had the same kind of coughing fit when I woke up too."

They were still underground, that much she could tell. But the cavern they were in seemed more welcoming, less sinister and dark. Abruptly, Silvia noticed Hira seated a few feet away with her feet tucked under her magnificent dress, and her slender hands folded neatly in her lap.

The Daughter of the Dragonfly Keeper, though tiny in stature, was extremely majestic. She held her head high and her back straight. The ever-flowing pink hair of hers twisted eerily around her pale shoulders as if it were alive.

"*Dhanyabaad*, Silvia." Hira said bowing her forehead to the rocky ground. "Thank you for saving my life."

Silvia was speechless. She looked at Manuela, who shrugged her shoulders. "You're Welcome, Hir ... Your Highness." Silvia mumbled.

"Kripayaa, please, call me Hira. I am honored to have you and your sister join our war against Shatru." Hira's hushed voice was like the tinkle of a wind chime from a light summer breeze.

Shaking the grogginess from her head, Silvia turned to Manuela. "Where's Fritz? Manu, what happened?" she said as she felt her chest tightening in fear.

"My eyes were closed until I heard that ... voice. Then I felt Fritz tear away and jump, so I opened my eyes in time to see him block some kind of dart from hitting you." Manuela lowered her eyes. "That's it. Then I felt like something sucked my breath away and I woke up coughing like you. Hira was here, and she helped me. You woke up right after that."

Fritz was gone. Silvia covered her face and cried. She cried from the deepest pit inside her. Manuela put her arms around her and Silvia could feel her trembling as well.

"I do not believe they will harm him ... yet," Hira said softly.

Silvia wiped her face on her muddy sleeve. "What did you say?"

"They will keep him just as they keep Jiwan. They will use him to stop you from continuing your quest."

"Are you saying that he's still alive?" Manuela asked, letting go of Silvia.

Hira nodded slightly. "Yes. This I know. I too saw the dart. It was *not* one to kill. Dushta's intent was obviously to capture." Silvia stared into the silvery-grey eyes and believed her.

Hira stood and her dress spread out, millions of iridescent sparkles sprinkling into the darkness of the cave. Now Silvia knew why she felt different in this cavern than the first one they had encountered; Hira's presence had transformed the gloomy dripping stalactites and monstrous cold stalagmites into rainbow-tinted carvings which reflected in the underground pool on the far side of the cathedral-sized cave.

"We need to find where Shatru is keeping Jiwan. That is where Fritz will be," Hira said with a determined look that didn't go with her fragile-looking body. Her gossamer wings were neatly folded down her back like a lustrous waterfall tinged by an evening sunset.

Manuela looked up at Hira. "But we have the maps. Only we don't know how to read them."

Hira started. She bent down immediately when Manuela pulled the thin book out of her pack. "How did you get this?" she demanded, scanning page after page with hungry eyes. Her face lit up like moonlight. "But this is exactly what we need!" she said excitedly.

When she was almost to the end, she smoothed out one of the crackly maps and stuck her finger right in the center of the maze-like markings. "Here it is!"

"You can read this?" Silvia asked amazed.

"Of course. These maps are lost mandalas written lifetimes ago by the first DragonFly Keeper. The DragonFlies at that time were not worried about anyone stealing the magic. These manuals were records of the secret places the DragonFlies dwelled." Hira traced the smudgy markings in curlycue patterns until her index finger stopped at the far left of the mandala. "Now, however, many of these places have long since been forgotten as the DragonFly

Keepers have had to keep more and more to sheltered places."

Silvia coughed again, and when she saw that her canteen was empty, she got up to fill it from the pool a few yards away. Her skirt was stiff with dried mud and she just now noticed how her shoes were covered with it. When she got to the pool, she noticed that light shone down from a shaft from far above.

"Where are we? What were you thinking of when you said three, Manu?" Silvia asked, staring at her ragged expression in the shadowy water.

"I guess I was thinking about Fritz. This place doesn't look like anything I'd dream up as safe."

Hira smiled and, after waving her hand in a soft motion, put a finger to her lips. She seemed to taste something. "We are far away from Huri and his animals. I'd say we are close to Crystal Mountain."

"Crystal Mountain?" Silvia filled her canteen and sipped the ice cold water. "That sounds like a ride at Disney World."

"Crystal Mountain is where Jiwan is. Crystal Mountain is an ancient long forgotten place where few people ever go. Deep in a hidden cave, Shatru has kept watch over the world." Hira's hair sparkled with energy as she strode over to Silvia with the *Tala Pahaad*. Manuela walked over to the cool water to refill her canteen as well.

"But if you knew where Jiwan was, why didn't you just go to Crystal Mountain in the first place?" asked Manuela.

"Because we didn't know how to find the hidden cave. Until now. This mandala that you have uncovered shows the secret, and therefore safe, route to the center of the earth." Hira reached out and put the closed book back in Manuela's backpack.

"We're going to the center of the earth?" Silvia asked shivering. The cave they were in was extremely cold and their tattered, dirty clothing was anything but warm.

Hira smiled that other-worldly smile and bent her head slightly to the side. "Not until nightfall tomorrow. It is Thursday morning. Tomorrow is *sukrabaar*, Friday. I will be able to have things ready for that time."

Hira left the two girls for a minute to fly to the opening above and assess their exact location. She told them that she would take them to a place to clean up, eat and rest when she returned.

Silvia sat with her back against a rock and stared at the silent pool of water. Manuela's stomach was growling and her eyes were sunken and flat. Silvia guessed she looked the same. She sure felt the same. *The center of the earth. That has to be worse than the mouth of a volcano. The center of the earth with the king of the Rogs. How can we ever help in a place like that?* She slumped over and pressed her fists into her hungry middle. Manuela didn't say anything but sat staring into the water lost in her own thoughts.

When Hira returned, she shook snow from her translucent wings. "I was right. We are in Nepal, in the Himalayas," she said smiling. "The DragonFlies originated here when this area was an island in a dark blue ocean."

"Aren't the Himalayas the biggest mountains on earth?" Silvia asked, eyes wide.

"They are now. A long, long time ago this area was an ocean." Hira shook out the snowflakes from the folds in her webby dress. "Crystal Mountain has long been sacred even to people. It is almost as if some people can still feel the magic under all the ice and snow. Now who has the *shaanti?* You must have one to have found the Demon-King's army. For now we will go and get you two cleaned up and fed. When you have rested, I shall tell you more." Hira waited while Silvia pulled out the small stone and handed it to Manuela.

"These words will take you to the place we are going only once. You should be honored to know that no humans have ever been there, so don't be alarmed at the initial reception the DragonFlies will give you." Hira paused while Manuela and Silvia got up, shouldered their packs, and held hands. Silvia felt the absence of Fritz in her empty left hand.

When their eyes were closed, Hira started intoning the phrase Manuela would have to say to take them there. *Bayaa tira jaanos. Dayaa tira jaanos. Sidhaa jaanos.* It seemed to Silvia as if Hira's tinkling voice repeated this string of words fifty times before there was silence. A moment later Manuela's tired and cracked voice tried out the words in a halting manner: *Bayaa tira jaanos. Dayaa tira jaanos. Sidhaa jaanos.*

Chapter 23

Manuela discovers chang

EVEN BEFORE OPENING HER EYES, Manuela inhaled the fragrant air and sighed. So much had happened in the last few days that the cinnamon-scented air that reminded her of Miss Sasha made her feel as if she had been on a journey for many months. When she did finally open her eyes, she stared in wonder.

All around them the tropical glade they were in was lit up with sunlight. About the size of a city block, the glade was filled with DragonFly soldiers and other DragonFlies of different colors. Some were as red as cherries and carried baskets of breads and other foods up to a raised platform at one end of the clearing. Their garments flowed like fire behind them as they glided out of the jungle and from nearby fires with their loads of food. Giant trees ringed the edge of the clearing and many were weighted down with mangos and other strange fruit. Soldiers stood with icy gazes and long thin spears next to the trees.

Although the clearing was teeming with activity, it was strangely silent. Apart from the soft swish of the grass as they passed, and the clink of metal and thud of wood, the DragonFlies made no sound at all. If it weren't for their serene and sparkling faces, Manuela would have thought they were preparing for a funeral.

At the end opposite the platform, golden DragonFlies with umber wings were circling a smoking fire. The air carried the scent of slowly simmering pumpkin and apple cider. They lifted giant platters of vegetables and bowls of steaming stew and gave them to the cherry-colored carriers. Then they bent back to sacks of vibrantly colored orange and yellow spices and sprinkled them into the iron skillets set on racks over the low fire.

When they first appeared, no one seemed to take special notice. But when the soldier DragonFlies noticed that Hira was accompanied by tall, dirty, fleshy human girls with their long dark curly hair springing out in every direction, they immediately circled them and crossed their spears, locking them inside.

After raising her arms and making some strange movements and saying something in her unfamiliar language, the guards uncrossed their spears and bowed to the girls.

"I told them that you were our guests because you saved my life at the battle with Huri. They know we are in your debt and that you choose to help us again." Hira motioned for the girls to follow her.

She glided to a far corner of the glade where beautifully white-robed DragonFly women with flowing white hair were waiting in a line. While most of the DragonFlies seemed genderless, these were obviously female by their more curvy figures. They bowed low before Hira and just stared at Manuela and Silvia.

"*Bahini Taaja,*" Hira said, addressing the tallest and most beautiful of the attendants. "These, too, are our sisters. They have risked their lives and brought me the mandala which will take us to Jiwan. Please offer them your assistance." Then she turned to Manuela and Silvia and said, "I need to go now and speak with my guards. These attendants will take care of you until we feast tonight." And with that, she strode off to speak with some of the soldiers.

"Hi, I'm Silvia," Silvia said smiling and holding out her hand. The DragonFly Hira had called Taaja grabbed her dirty hand and shook her head disapprovingly. She pulled Silvia to a path that led into the jungle. Other attendants took hold of Manuela's arms and ushered her in as well.

"I know we don't smell very good, but they sure have a strange way of introducing themselves." Silvia said as they were led to a deep clear pool amid tall jungle ferns and papaya trees.

Manuela didn't care. She was so happy to take a relaxing bath and put the search for the Keeper on hold for a day. Then she felt terribly guilty as she thought of Fritz imprisoned by the disgusting Rogs. *Don't worry Fritz. We will gather our strength here with Hira and we will come and get you,* she thought.

The girls were cleaned and oiled and dressed gently by the attendants, who even gave them massages. After braiding their hair in multiple braids, they tied them off with tiny gold thread. Then they brought out long white cotton tunics and pants and then light grey fur pants and tunics to go over them. Taaja put the heavy fur tunics aside and showed them how to belt their cotton tunics with a thick purple cord. Finally, the attendants brought out two pairs of shoes for each of them. They slipped a pair of soft brown leather sandals on their feet and left heavily furred grey boots by the other heavier clothing.

"I'm not so sure I really want to go to a place that cold," Silvia said, eying the elaborate fur tunics. They had built in mittens and a hood with a mouth scarf.

"If it means getting Fritz back, I will go anywhere," Manuela said getting up and walking away. She knew she probably hurt Silvia's feelings; if anyone missed Fritz and would risk her life for him it was Silvia. But she was so angry at the Rogs and Shatru, and she felt so guilty just sitting here waiting for a feast. She didn't want to be reminded of that.

The attendants led the girls back to the glade and motioned for them to sit down with them and wait. Manuela noticed Silvia's sullen look but Silvia wouldn't meet her gaze and sat down at the edge of the group, away from Manuela. *Oh, get over it,* she thought. *We finally made it to the DragonFlies and Hira, and I'm not going to fight now.*

From where they were, they had a good view of the platform and its preparations. Baskets of large orange, purple, red and yellow flowers were being thrown on and around woven mats laid out in a circle. Then wooden platters were laid down in front of the mats and the bright red DragonFlies placed honey-colored braided bread on each platter. Next, they placed small wooden cups by the platters and filled them with a buttery-cinnamon smelling tea. Manuela's mouth watered at the scent floating over and she had the impulse to turn to Silvia and comment, but when she looked at her sister sitting by herself at the opposite side of the attendants, she couldn't get her eye.

Suddenly, amidst all the preparation, three guards started blaring on thin trumpets. The eerie wail they made sent shivers up Manuela's spine. When they heard this, all the DragonFlies stopped what they were doing and stood facing the guards. After lowering their instruments, the guards parted and Hira walked through and up to the platform amidst the bowed heads of the other DragonFlies. Her pale pink hair was braided and tied up in an elaborate crown on her head with dark purple ribbons. Her dress, almost translucent in its iridescence, floated in waves behind her, yet was still open in the front up to her upper thigh, allowing her lean silvery legs to climb the steps up to the platform easily.

While the beauty of her dress alone was mesmerizing, what made Manuela stare in awe were her DragonFly wings. Fully open and outstretched they seemed to match her height, which was a little shorter than Silvia. Their delicate silver veins pulsed rhythmically causing them to shimmer like miniature sapphire waves caught in the last orange rays of a setting sun. Hira held them open regally, and there was no doubt she was in charge in the Keeper's absence.

After Hira sat on the central mat, the white attendants quickly got up and ushered Manuela and Silvia onto the platform and to the woven mats on either side of Hira. Then they all went back down, except for Taaja, who sat down next to Manuela. In an orderly, formal fashion, more important looking DragonFlies of different colors and sizes joined them on the platform. During this assembling, Hira sat with her hands solemnly in her lap, and everyone followed her example.

When everyone was seated and the rest of the DragonFlies were ringing the platform grouped by color, Hira raised her cup above her head.

"We are gathered here to give thanks for life. To eat from nature's bounty and continue the cycle of hope and community." She gulped the steaming tea in one swig and then set it down. "May we all find peace and strength for our final struggle."

Everyone raised their glasses and gulped down their tea, so Manuela quickly grabbed hers and tilted back her head. It was smooth and warm. Although it had a bitter and strong taste, it was mellowed by a sweet and buttery aftertaste that reminded Manuela of cinnamon rolls.

"Welcome our new sisters Silvia and Manuela, who have joined our battle to free Jiwan and restore the Magic to Earth." Hira took the girls' hands when she said this and raised them in front of their faces.

"*Swaagat,*" the group of DragonFlies said in unison. Their many voices sounded like water falling down a stony slope, a light washing of sound that left Manuela with goose bumps.

"And now we eat!" Hira smiled, and all the DragonFlies let out cheers and began chattering in their unfamiliar tongue. Manuela was so startled at their change from silence to chaotic mumbling that she forgot that she was still holding Hira's hand. When Hira finally opened her fingers to pull her hand back, Manuela felt silly. But Hira smiled at her warmly and squeezed her hand before letting it go.

"I am sure that you two will love our food. We usually follow the traditional ways of the people living here in the Himalaya Mountains, but some of our recipes are secret to the DragonFlies and give strength and peace in ways only our magic can provide," she said with an excited grin that crinkled up her nose in an almost childlike way.

"This bread is delicious!" Silvia said as she pulled apart the braids of the still steaming roll left on her platter.

Manuela sighed as she saw how the food had made Silvia forget about her anger, and she happily bit into her crusty loaf. It was warm and tasted of roasted garlic.

When she looked up, she saw lines of the fiery-red Dragonflies dishing out various things onto the wooden platters, starting with Hira and then some moving to Silvia and others moving to Manuela until everyone seated had platters and bowls filled and steaming. Not knowing where to begin, Manuela stared at the dumplings and curries and hesitated.

"I always like to start with the dumplings," Taaja said softly, leaning over towards Manuela, "We call them *Mo Mo*, and they are filled with cabbage and cauliflower and wild turkey."

Manuela picked up one of the dumplings and smelled it. It had that faint cinnamon smell and looked slick and white. Carefully she tasted it and her eyes lit up. Then her eyes grew wide and she reached for the water one of the servers had poured.

Taaja laughed. "That was probably the chili you tasted. What did you think?"

"It's … wonderful. It tasted like a wild rainy spring day in an overgrown orchard."

"That's the turmeric and cumin. Those spices are very earthy." Taaja pointed to a thick black soup. "Try the *gundruk ko jhol.*"

With a thick pewter spoon, Manuela stirred the black mixture and then brought some of the chunky acid smelling liquid to her mouth. Taaja laughed when she made a face and forced herself to swallow.

"I guess that one's not your favorite."

"What's *in* that? It tastes like rotten mud with chunks." Manuela reached for the water again.

"Well, *gundruk* is dried old fermented mustard leaves. I suppose its earthiness is something you must get used to."

"What's this? It smells sweet," Manuela said pointing to a pretty mound of vegetables.

"Oh! That's one of my favorites, *chyau alu ko tarkari*. It's potatoes, mushrooms, onions and tomatoes all together. Try it."

Manuela used her spoon, after wiping it off on some bread, and scooped up the fragrant stew. The intense flavor exploded in her mouth. "Mmmm. That's the best vegetable stew I've ever had."

Taaja continued helping Manuela decipher her food while they ate and laughed. They ate pumpkin vine tips sautéed in butter, fried bamboo shoots, plantain curry and spicy almond chicken with raisins and honey. They ate quail with cloves, rhubarb chutney with cinnamon and, when she thought she would burst, the DragonFlies brought creamy white coconut fudge. During the whole meal, Manuela washed everything down with the salty buttery tea and chai, a sweeter tea. After the coconut fudge, her cup was filled with a slightly effervescent pale milky brew with a tangy flavor that Taaja called *chang*.

"Be careful with that. Too much can make you feel sick," Taaja said, arching her eyebrows as Manuela drank the whole cup in one go.

During the meal, Silvia had been talking with Hira. While Manulea had enjoyed Taaja's company, she felt a little left out as she kept glancing at them leaning together. Silvia had eaten well as usual by the look of her plate, but

Hira seemed to have eaten only a bite of everything. Finally, Hira happened to look her way as Manuela was facing her direction.

"I hope you find our feast filling and Taaja good company," Hira said smiling.

"Oh yes, I was starving after our chase in the Congo. This mountain food is really good." Manuela started to sip the fresh cup of *chang* that had been poured for her.

"I think these girls are wonderful, Hira," Taaja said. "I feel very lucky that we have joined to finish the search for Jiwan. Silvia, did you enjoy your meal?"

"I think my favorite dessert is now coconut fudge," Silvia said between mouthfuls. She looked from Taaja to Manuela and smiled sheepishly.

Thank goodness for good food, thought Manuela. She smiled back at Silvia and finished off her *chang*. She really was starting to feel pretty good.

Hira rose and walked to the center of the circled DragonFlies and the chatter died down immediately. Her other-worldly smile softened the painful look in her eyes.

"This feast is to celebrate the hope we have for the safe return of Jiwan. Never before in DragonFly history have we had to endure so much pain and opposition. It is time to set aside all feelings of peace until Jiwan comes home." The Dragonflies' eyes all locked on to Hira with an intensity that gave Manuela goose bumps. Her stomach tightened when one blue-silver guard gazed directly at her before locking on to Hira's. "Now we must go prepare ourselves for the ordeal of this homecoming. We must be prepared never to return home without Jiwan."

When Hira said this the DragonFlies smiles completely faded and their jaws set into hard expressions. She looked up into the darkening sky and raised her arms high over her head.

"TO WAR!" she screamed so loudly that the trees rattled.

"To war! To war!" echoed the DragonFlies. Silvia and Manuela raised their fist and chanted along with Taaja and the rest, fearful of the fire in their eyes. The shouting stopped as Hira stepped down off the platform and the DragonFlies silently filed down the stairs to their different posts. Taaja turned toward the girls as they stood and motioned for an attendant to come to the stairs.

"Jaado will take you to a place to rest. When you are hungry come back to the grove and you can eat," Taaja said in a hurried distracted manner. Then without a 'good bye' or 'nice to meet you,' she strode off the platform to join Hira.

Jaado met them as they came off the steps and offered them silky white scarves to wrap around their shoulders for the air had begun to get chilly. A slight breeze blew their loose cotton pants around as they followed her silently down a path into the jungle. After only a few paces, Jaado stopped and pointed to a tent made out of a thin green cloth, which hung from the branches and draped over large bushes and boulders. Then she pressed her hands together and bowed at them without a word and quickly turned and ran back up the path, her white wings rippling like rainbows in the moonlight.

Chapter 24

Manuela steps off the path

SILVIA WAS WALKING ALL AROUND the house looking for her backpack. Her mom had already gone out to the car with Manuela and was waiting to take them to school. *Where did I put it? Where could it be?* She felt a breeze and looked around the living room trying to figure out where it came from. All the windows were closed. *Where is that backpack?* She picked up a black couch cushion and jumped back. Snakes started piling out and slithering across the floor. "Ahhhhh! AHHHHHHH!"

"Wake up, Silvia! Wake up!" Manuela was shaking her and she sat bolt upright and looked around rubbing her eyes. Thin gauzy cloth the color of grasshoppers flowed above them in a slight breeze.

"Oh, Manuela. It was awful. The snakes ..." Silvia rubbed her arms and shuddered.

"Don't talk about it, Silvi. If you don't talk about it, then it will be easier to forget. Come on. I don't know why after that feast last night, but I am really hungry."

Silvia stretched and followed Manuela out of the tent. Various colored DragonFlies passed by on the trail leading back towards the clearing. After pausing by a small pool of fresh water next to the tent which had two clean snow-white towels laid out for them, they joined the flow of traffic.

Silvia and Manuela walked side by side crunching the tender green shoots that poked out of the loamy path. "Manu, I'm glad you're here."

Manuela turned and looked at her oddly and then smiled. Putting her arm around Silvia she squeezed her shoulders slightly. "We'll find Fritz. We will. And we'll save Jiwan. I know why Miss Sasha picked you. You won't give up until you win." She smiled at Silvia and pulled on one of the gold-threaded braids.

"And it's a good thing too, or we'd still be covered in stinky mud looking for a grandpa bird," Silvia laughed. Manuela rolled her eyes and let go of her shoulders as they entered the clearing. Silvia tried not to smile too much but secretly she felt elated. Somehow she and Manuela had begun to really talk. At the clearing, the girls followed the DragonFlies to the far side where the golden DragonFlies were busy around a fire. Strangely, after the feast the night before, Silvia was starving this morning as well. She could smell a sweet buttery scent and the warm yeasty fragrance of fresh bread wafted over from the hot griddles that the golden DragonFlies were working on.

"*Namaste*," a tall, white robed DragonFly woman said, bowing slightly as she stepped in front of them. "Hira asked me to greet you. She is busy with the preparations and will be with you at the mid-afternoon meal." Silvia wondered what types of 'preparations' Hira was making. As much as she wanted to save Fritz and Jiwan, the actual thought of participating in a battle like the one yesterday made her shiver. Until this morning, everything had just seemed like a crazy dream. It felt as if she and Manuela and Fritz were starring in some great movie and the fear and danger were not really real. But this morning as she sat cross-legged next to Manuela and their DragonFly companion, she realized that, even though she breathed magic with every breath, she very likely could leave that breath at Crystal Mountain tomorrow. And if they lost, maybe that would be the best place to leave it.

"Silvia, are you alright? You haven't touched your breakfast." Silvia looked down at her wooden plate filled with hot flat bread and raspberry compote.

"I'm fine, Manu. It's just, well ... Aren't you worried about tonight at all?"

Manuela sighed and picked at her bread. "Of course. But we're here for a reason, right? I mean, Miss Sasha wouldn't have chosen us if we weren't going to make it." Silvia met her eyes and didn't say anything. Their DragonFly friend got up to get them more *poecha*, or buttered tea. When she was a few steps away, Manuela gave Silvia a stern look. "Come on, Silvi. Don't get like this now. You're the one who *isn't* supposed to brood on the terrible possibilities. That's my job," she said with a smirk.

Silvia burst out laughing, her tension fading away. "Oh well, I suppose you will worry enough for both of us." She picked up some of the flatbread and swirled and smashed it in the salty weak tea. "You know, Manu, if you ignore the weird smell, this sort of tastes like eating warm cookie dough."

"If you say so. I've never eaten your cookie dough." Manuela ate her bread without dipping it in the tea. "You know, Silvia, no one is going to believe we ate breakfast with DragonFlies."

Silvia tilted her head thoughtfully. "Yes, that's true. But I think it only matters if *we* believe."

Their companion's name was Sangeet, which meant music. They soon found that all of the DragonFlies had names that meant something important. Like Native Americans, their names were chosen when they finished their childhood and entered the strangely ageless ranks of DragonFlies, keepers of faith and hope in the world. Sangeet was more talkative than the other Dragonflies they had met and her ice-blue eyes had a different sparkle. She seemed to be talking with them when she glanced your way.

After breakfast, she had led them down another winding path into the dense forest. They had sucked on fresh mangoes while Sangeet told them a little about the DragonFly hierarchy. The Keeper, or Jiwan, was like a king, except he didn't order the other DragonFlies to do things at all. Instead, the Keeper was seen as an eternal president. He was respected and revered but also just like all the other DragonFlies. Being the Keeper was passed on to children. Children were rare. How they came about, Sangeet didn't say, but they were cared for by purple DragonFlies. It seemed that DragonFlies had jobs in accordance with their color. The yellow and burnt-umber DragonFlies were the cooks, the red ones were carriers, and the white ones, which seemed female, were healers. When there wasn't anyone to heal, they talked with various DragonFlies and tried to heal their spirits, if needed.

Silvia used the back of her hand to wipe some juice which was dribbling off her chin. She was fascinated by the things Sangeet was telling them. She had so many questions. After only a few, though, Manuela had kicked her in the calf. Sangeet never answered her questions anyway; she just kept on telling them other fascinating things about her society. Soon they stepped into a clearing the size of a large parking lot that was rimmed with red poppies. In the center was a raised black stone, smooth and shiny in the sun.

"What is that?" Manuela asked as she stepped through the poppies towards the stone which was about their height.

"ROKNU! STOP!" Sangeet's soft musical voice came out like a hot flame. Manuela paused with her foot in the air and stumbled backwards as Sangeet grabbed her by the purple cord around her tunic. Silvia dropped her mango.

"What's wrong?" Silvia asked as Manuela looked down at her feet. Her wooden sandals were smoking.

"*Yo mero galti ho.* Dear Manuela, it is my fault." Sangeet said softly as she bent down to see Manuela's feet. Her yellow-tinged wings swept out along the path enclosing them like a cloud. "I forgot. This field cannot be entered unless you are of our realm."

"Your realm?" Manuela asked as she winced. Sangeet had taken off Manuela's sandals and was rubbing something oily onto her singed feet. Silvia stared through the yellow film of Sangeet's wings at the shiny black stone and then down at the red soles of Manuela's feet.

"What I mean is that no humans can enter here. It looks like a field to you, but to us it is a locus of energy. We can see it … differently. On another plane. We find the *shaantis* here." Sangeet finished and stood up straight, folding her wings back like a toss of blonde hair. She took their hands and led them back the way they came. Her light manner was gone. Her icy eyes looked straight ahead. "Don't worry, Manuela. Your feet are fine. They will tingle for another hour and then it will stop."

Silvia looked down at Manuela's bare feet. They were no longer red and she seemed to be walking on the rough path without pain. But why did Sangeet seem afraid? If everything was truly alright, why were her eyes closed off and cold?

Re-entering the main clearing, Sangeet quickly bowed to them and passed them off to two silent white DragonFlys who didn't say a word to Sangeet. They watched her go off unsmiling and sat down cross-legged and spoke to each other in their strange language.

"What's going on?" Silvia asked Manuela quietly. All the DragonFlies had stopped what they were doing and were watching Sangeet cross the clearing towards a corner of the stern blue DragonFlies.

Manuela looked around. "Something's happened. I did something terrible, I think." She closed her eyes and bowed her head.

"What do you mean? It wasn't *your* fault. You didn't know that would happen. What even happened anyway?" Silvia whispered just like the two DragonFlies who seemed to be ignoring them, although Silvia could tell they were watching the two girls out the corner of their eyes.

"No, but I did something terrible anyway. And now I think Sangeet is going to pay for it." Manuela sat down and covered her face with her hands. Silvia didn't know what to say so she sat down next to her and put her arm around her while they waited for something to happen.

Finally, Hira emerged into the clearing with a group of blue DragonFlies. She walked elegantly over to the two girls, who got up along with the rest of the DragonFlies. She didn't look angry, but she wasn't smiling either. Very softly she laid her hands on the girls' shoulders. "I'm sorry, but there will be no mid-afternoon meal. We must leave now for the Crystal Mountain."

"Hira, what's going on? What did I do?" Manuela asked on the edge of tears.

Hira squeezed their shoulders. "All magic has access to the energy poles. Unknowingly, you have disturbed the energy and now this area will be easy for the Rogs to find. Our preparations are already final. We go now. You will be taken to Whisperer's Glen where we will meet." Hira turned and raised her hands to the sky. In a loud voice she spoke to them in their language and they answered with shrill cries. Then she quickly disappeared into the fringe of the forest.

The two quiet DragonFlies led them back to the area where their grey tunics were waiting. After stuffing the fur into the tops of her boots, Silvia stood up and wiped the sweat from her forehead. None of the DragonFlies were dressing. They were busy dismantling tents.

"I feel like it is my fault no one gets to eat," Manuela said with a sigh. She and Silvia stood waiting to be led to Whisperer's Glen.

"We'll eat," Silvia said. "You saw the bags of lumpy bread and other things they were packing into bags. No one seems to be treating us any differently. Don't worry about it now. Let's get ready to find Fritz."

Manuela nodded, and then they were being led away down another endless path tangled with vines and roots. They were completely surrounded by DragonFlies, some white and some blue. There would be no stepping off the path this time.

Chapter 25

Whisperer's Glen

WHISPERER'S GLEN WAS QUIET. The clearing was broken up by clumps of tall vine-tangled trees which blocked the light and let in strange breezes from the mountains beyond. Hira greeted them more warmly this time, smiling and leading them by hand toward an opening to the north, towards the mountains. Blue DragonFlies were already entering the shadowy tunnel in the trees.

Manuela looked around at the liquid colors of the DragonFly wings flashing and mixing. The rainbow kaleidoscope was making her dizzy. She chewed on a strange gummy cube of cheese that Hira had given each of them. *Where was Sangeet?* She hadn't seen her since the walk and was too nervous to ask Hira about it. *Do I really want to know anyway?* She thought. *Yes. I do.* Manuela followed behind Silvia, a blue DragonFly stepping quietly behind her. *I must do something to make up for what I did,* she thought, chewing rapidly.

"Do you think this cheese-gum would go over well back in Ohio?" Silvia said over her shoulder. Manuela spit hers out into her hand and shoved it in the pocket of her tunic quickly.

"Do *you* think 'old cheese' is a great flavor for gum?" Manuela said into her sister's ear. They were going slowly and single file up a steep winding incline. Although the temperature seemed cooler, the constant climbing kept them sweating in their furs. The DragonFlies seemed impervious to the temperature no matter what it was.

They marched silently for hours. Manuela was starting to get hungry. So much walking over the last few days had given her an appetite. *How can Silvi stand to feel like this all the time?* she wondered. Just as her stomach let out a sinister growl, she heard a DragonFly up ahead call out "ROKNU!" Manuela had no trouble remembering that meant 'stop.' Silvia, however, bumped into a tall red DragonFly in front of her who turned around in surprise.

"Sorry, sorry. Sorry about that," she said sheepishly. The red DragonFly smiled and handed both Silvia and Manuela flat bread and mangoes from a thin red sling that all red DragonFlies carried around their slim waists.

"Thank you," Manuela said softly and bowed her head. The Dragonfly didn't speak but bowed in return and turned around to eat with the DragonFly in front.

The girls munched the bread and took a look at the scenery. It was definitely starting to get chilly. In the distance, through evergreen trees and brush, Manuela could see mountains looming into the sky like sharp teeth, white and shiny in the sun. She had never seen such huge mountains in real life. One of them held Fritz and Jiwan and a group of devils and monsters. She shuddered and put the rest of the bread and her mango in her backpack, suddenly loosing her appetite.

Before long they were marching again, and the girls settled into their own thoughts until the sun starting sliding down the sky on their left. All around them the ground was covered in a layer of snow and their footsteps were muffled. The mountains spread before them like pink and lavender cotton candy. A fiery orange peeked out of the "V" of two mountains and cut a line across the valley to their left. They were on a ridge which curled around another mountain.

"That is so amazing," Siliva said. Manuela had to catch her as she almost slipped off the trail.

"Silvia! Be careful."

"Alright, alright. I just can't believe how the center of evil could be inside so much beauty." Silvia took her eyes from the lemon and tangerine shadows as the DragonFlies marched a few paces sharply to their right.

"I think we're stopping or something," Manuela said as they ducked under a few snow laden branches. They were in a big clearing that slanted up the mountain with the DragonFlies gathered in a circle. They seemed to be grouped according to color. Manuela looked up at the pattern their colored wings made against the snowy slope. The outside was a ring of rose-colored wings and long flowing magenta hair. Standing in small clumps all around the group, creamy white DragonFlies blended into the snow around them, reflecting the soft evening glow. Cobalt blue shimmered amid burnt-umber and red and yellow which flashed in the heavy melon-colored light. In the inner rings, beautiful plumper DragonFlies that Manuela had never seen before held hands as their sea foam hair flowed out around them.

They had long sage-colored dresses that curled around on the ground around them covering their feet unlike the other DragonFlies. On a rugged stone in the middle stood Hira. Silver light seemed to reflect off her hair like starlight and her pale arms glowed like amethyst as she held them above her head in the glow of the setting sun.

Hira began to chant slowly in an ethereal voice in her own language. When she finished there was no sound except for an eagle screeching overhead. Suddenly other screeches stretched across the sky, getting louder and louder. The DragonFlies looked up in confusion and then let out war cries and began scattering into formations. Manuela turned around and saw at least two dozen huge grey bats with long snakelike tails descending on them. Silvia screamed and threw her arms around Manuela and the two, already too close to the edge, tumbled down the steep bank.

Chapter 26

Manuela gets very, very cold

EVEN THROUGH THE FURS, Manuela could feel the tingling cold. She hadn't tried to open her eyes yet, but her face felt far away anyway. She knew they had fallen, but she couldn't tell if it had just ended or if she had been laying there for a long time. She couldn't even tell if she *was* lying down or standing up. It was if she were floating softly through the air. She was ... so ... sleepy...

"Manu!"

What was that? The cry seemed so tiny and far away. *Silvia?* She couldn't get herself to open her eyes, or even move her head. It was almost as if she didn't have a body anymore but was just a breeze. A breeze ... floating ... softly ...

"Manu!"

Silvia? Where are you? Suddenly she knew she at least had a head because it hurt. The pain was sharp and unbearable like a knife slapping ... her face?

"Manu!"

Silvia! I hear you! Silvi, where am I? Help! Silvia's voice seemed louder but muffled, as if she were underwater.

"Please, Manu, wake up, wake up!"

Silvia, I hear you! I'm awake! I'm awake! I can't remember where my mouth is. I don't know how to move. Silvia, help me! Don't leave me here! Then the pain was unbearable, screaming so loudly that she couldn't hear Silvia's voice anymore. The pain pressed on her like the end of a hot cane. And then it was gone, and everything was spinning … spinning … spinning …

Silvia kept rubbing Manuela's cheeks and calling out her name. But it was no use. She wouldn't wake up. She was alive; Silvia knew because her tiny breath left a faint fog right under her nose. But she wouldn't wake up.

After the terrifying sight of the winged bats with their red eyes, Silvia had jumped onto Manuela not thinking, and they had tumbled down the slope separately, banging into bushes and getting poked by jagged rocks. It was like getting beat up on all sides at the same time. Silvia had curled up into a ball and covered her head. When it was over, she didn't move at first. Her ears were ringing and her mouth tasted like metal. When she did open her eyes, she could see the pink snow by her mouth in the fading light. Far above she could hear screeches and screams. Quickly she closed her eyes and curled up, covering her ears.

Finally, there was silence, and, when she opened her eyes again, darkness. There was no moonlight or starlight and it was *cold*. At first she had tried whispering Manuela's name, hoping that she was nearby and asleep. But after a few times, she grew worried. She began crawling around on all fours trying to feel for something. The slope seemed to have leveled off and she had been caught by a gnarly bush. She began calling more loudly until she could hear the echoes of her cries around her. Still silence.

Although the cold made her sleepy, she knew enough not to stop moving, and tried to stand up. After a few dizzy spills, she was able to stay up. She jumped on one foot and then the other to make sure nothing was broken. Then she began stumbling around in the darkness. Suddenly the cloud cover drew back and a half-moon spilled cool light down onto the snow. Silvia jumped at her own shadow and fell over shaking. Then she started laughing hysterically. No matter how hard she tried she couldn't stop, and she couldn't stand up again. She was in shock. So she rolled slowly away from the bush towards a tree and, still laughing so hard it hurt, she pulled herself up, and then stopped with her mouth open. On the other side of the tree Manuela was almost face down in a dark splotch of snow.

After turning her over, Silvia wiped the blood off her sister's face and brushed the snow away from her eyes and mouth. She had tried shaking her and rubbing her cheek to wake her up. But no matter how loud she cried, Manuela lay limp in her arms.

Brushing away tears, Silvia pulled out both their blankets and wrapped them around Manuela's head and shoulders. She found the mango in Manuela's pack and tried to put some drops of the sweet juice into her sister's mouth. But it just dribbled down her cheek. Finally, holding her in her arms, Silvia placed her head on Manuela's chest and hugged her tightly, closing her eyes to troubled dreams.

When she woke up, the sun was already in the sky and warming her back. She sat up quickly and looked down to see Manuela staring up at her. Silvia's heart stopped. Manuela blinked and then blinked again.

"Manu! You're alive! I thought ... Say something!" Silvia propped Manuela up and unwrapped the blankets enough to grab one of Manuela's limp hands, which was as cold as the snow. One corner of Manuela's mouth twitched. Her dark eyes looked from Silvia to the tree and back again.

"C ... C ... C," she began. Silvia pulled some strands of hair out of Manuela's face. "C ... cold," she said softly and let out a sigh. Her mouth wouldn't smile, but Silvia could see her eyes trying to.

"I think that is the coldest you can get as a living human being and live to tell about it," said Silvia shakily. She propped Manuela up against the tree and watched her twitching strangely. She held up the mango and saw Manuela give an almost imperceptible nod of assent. While a lot of juice ran down her face, she was able to swallow some of it. After a few minutes she took a deep breath and shifted, moving her arms clumsily.

"N ... N ... Needles. Like needles," she said with a faint smile. Silvia thought of having to have your whole body tingling like it does when your arm or leg falls asleep. She grimaced with sympathy as Manuela jerked her legs and arms.

Finally, Manuela was rubbing her hands together and moving more smoothly. "What happened?"

Silvia told Manuela that it had been all night since they had fallen and everything had been silent.

"But we have to get back to Hira!" Manuela stammered in shock. Obviously, she hadn't realized how long she had been out.

"How, Manu. Can you even walk? And how can we climb all the way back up even if you could?"

"Well, we certainly can't just stay here," Manuela said as she tried to push herself over and stand up. She stumbled and fell face first in the snow.

"Manu!" Silvia helped her sister sit up again.

"I guess we will have to think of something else," Manuela said, wiping snow off her face. Silvia looked up the slope. They had fallen down 500 feet of rocky, snowy terrain. A few scrubby bushes and trees grew here and there, but for the most part nothing else grew on the mountainside. If only they could call loud enough to Hira.

"That's it!" Silvia shouted, standing up and grabbing Manuela's pack off her back. She began rummaging around frantically.

"What are you talking about? What are looking for in my pack?"

"Do you have any of Aru's crisps left? I had forgotten we had them." Silvia turned the backpack over. Amid the fallen clothes was the little package of crisps that Aru had given them. There was one left.

Manuela picked it up slowly and smiled. "Silvi, that's it! How could we have forgotten!" She began to eat, but then stopped. "Silvia," she said, holding the wafer out. You should do it this time. It was your idea anyway."

Silvia smiled happily, grabbed the crisp and popped it in her mouth. She felt the spicy cinnamon tang tingle her tongue as the crisp melted like warm honey. Suddenly she blinked. She thought she saw something out of the corner of her eye. Then she blinked again. The air was foggy and blue and suddenly two DragonFlies were standing in front of the girls with their spears at attention. No swarming group of pixies this time.

"Hira will be glad that you are well," the taller of the two said in a smooth voice. Their long straight hair sparkled like blue icicles in the morning sun. The two DragonFlies held out the shafts of their spears. "Close your eyes and hold on," said the tall one. "We will bring you back to her."

Silvia and Manuela took one last look around them and then at each other as they gathered their stuff and put in back in their packs. As they gripped the spears and closed their eyes, Silvia kept the image of the blue sky and white snow fixed in her mind as she prepared to meet Shatru at the center of the world.

Chapter 27

Crystal Mountain

THE TUNNEL WAS DARK, warm and smelled like Lake Erie after a bad storm. The slimy walls and floor were sticky and the dead fish smell seemed to get stronger as they descended down, down, down. A faint glow coming from the wings of the DragonFlies lit up the way. Instead of being way in the back, Manuela and Silvia had opened their eyes, after what seemed like a gust of wind, and saw that they were face to face with Hira. The DragonFly Keeper's daughter actually gasped in relief to see them and apologized for not properly looking after them. After that, they had been right at the front with her, slowly descending into the gut of the mountain.

"Crystal Mountain is not like anywhere else. Each stone vibrates with energy," Hira said softly. "Because the Rogs have been here, the energy manifests itself as this evil, disgusting slime." Her gossamer wings shuddered slightly letting off a faint whiff of honeysuckle in Silvia's face. Unfortunately, the fishy smell displaced it immediately.

"Hira," Silvia said, crinkling up her nose. "Won't Shatru sense we're coming and surprise us?"

"No, Silvia. Inside Crystal Mountain only the mountain can be seen. Our magic is consumed in the pulsing of the mountain. He will not be able to detect us that way." Hira stopped a moment at a fork in the tunnel and quickly chose the right. "If we move stealthily, using the map that you brought, we might be able to find the central chamber unnoticed."

They kept on in silence until Manuela gasped and stopped, grabbing Silvia's arm. "What was that?"

"What?"

"That weird sound. It was like a squeally growl." Manuela's eyes were wide and her hand was cold and sweaty.

"Manu," Silvia said as she opened her eyes wide. "I think what you just heard might be ..."

"There it was again!" Manuela cried. Hira cocked her head to one side and smiled. "What? What is it? Do you know, Hira?" Manuela looked from Silvia to Hira.

Silvia grabbed her sister by the shoulders. "Oh, no! Manu, I think it's the attack of the killer ... hunger! It was my stomach, you silly!" Silvia let go and doubled over laughing. Hira just looked at Manuela and smiled again, raising her eyebrow.

"O.K., O.K., only you would have a stomach that sounded like a wounded animal," Manuela said hotly. She was hungry herself, but she wasn't going to say anything. Perhaps the DragonFlies had eaten while they lay out there in the snow and had assumed that the girls had as well.

"When you are hungry, please just say," Hira said softly. "We eat more for ritual and forget that you need constant sustenance." She nodded, and a red DragonFly came forward with two large flatbreads and a thermos of the hot buttery tea. The girls thanked the red DragonFly, and Hira turned back towards the tunnel and they began to descend once more.

"She sure was right about you needing constant sustenance," Manuela whispered. "I'm surprised the Rogs didn't come running to attack at the sound of that stomach of yours."

"Not everyone is afraid of digestive noises, Manuela," Silvia whispered back, stifling a giggle.

After the bread and tea, Manuela felt a little better. She ached all over from the fall and the cold, however, and in the faint glow, she started to see black spots. *When are we going to rest? It seems like we've been marching for hours!* As if in response to her thoughts, Hira stopped at the next fork in the tunnel and turned around with her finger at her lips. With a quick jerk of her cotton candy hair, a group of blue DragonFlies pressed themselves against the wall and silently slipped in front of her along the wall of the right tunnel.

Hira placed one finger on her lips and with the other hand motioned for the girls to flatten themselves against the slimy wall. Silvia almost gagged, and Manuela had to keep from breathing through her nose to stand it. Then Hira went through a whole series of hand motions, and the DragonFlies glided silently around them and through the tunnel. When only the white DragonFlies were left, Hira grabbed Manuela by one hand and Silvia by the other and nodded for them to follow.

From the faint amber glow of Hira's wings, Manuela could see that the tunnel was getting larger and hotter.

As they tip-toed along the pebbly pathway, she saw that the slime was no longer covering the walls and she felt the dry crispness of the air which made her hair stand up on end. It had a burnt sulfur smell that was almost as bad as the fishy slime. The walls turned into ragged black cliffs; the ceiling of the cavern they were in reached two or three stories.

Gradually the silence was giving way to a strange rumbling that made the stones shift under their feet. Manuela could feel goose bumps crawling over her arms. Ahead, the other DragonFlies were assembled in the flickering shadows that a fire was casting.

Finally, they stepped into an enormous cavern and hid behind one of the many black boulders that were scattered around. Manuela's heart was pounding so hard, it felt like it would explode onto the ground. She could smell the Rogs and she realized the rumbling was the sound of the Rogs arguing in their coarse language.

"They seem too preoccupied with themselves and haven't figured out we are here." Hira pulled out two small vials from one of the silvery folds of her gown and handed them to the girls. "Take this and you will understand them."

Manuela took the small clear vial of golden liquid and drank it without hesitation. She expected it to be lemony like the cedru, but it was shockingly sweet like hot maple syrup. Suddenly, the rumbling started to make sense.

"… in the hole I tell you! Why bother keeping them alive?"

"I told you Runu, we need to lure the DragonFlies here to destroy them all. Who knows if they can come up with another Keeper?"

"I tell you they won't!" the first Rog named Runu screamed in a voice that seemed to gurgle. "Jiwan is the Keeper of their magic. If we get rid of him and these others, then we will have won!"

Manuela saw Silvia flinch and straighten up at the mention of "others." When Silvia got up and tried to peer around the boulder through some of the blue DragonFlies, Hira and Manuela followed.

"But Shatru told us to keep them there on that disc. If we throw them down the hole, he'll eat out our eyes and let the others chew off our limbs. They stay where they are, Runu."

Manuela could feel the heat in the stone as she gripped the boulder and looked around into a sulfurous cloud of smoke and flame. The first thing she noticed was Fritz. Silvia must have too, because she gripped Manuela's shoulder tightly with one hand and covered her mouth with the other. He was alive. But he was tied up with some strange glowing red twine that kept him from standing up or moving at all.

Fritz was next to Aru, Sir Luta, Alfio, and a golden DragonFly. Manuela bit her lip when she realized how narrowly they must have escaped being up there with them. All five were bound with the glowing red twine and sat back to back on a dark blue disc which hovered strangely over a giant hole belching the sulfurous smoke and flames.

"Is that Jiwan?" Silvia asked in a whisper. But Hira didn't answer. She was staring with watery eyes at the golden DragonFly. His head was bowed and his curly gold hair fell in flowing ringlets around his bound body. Manuela had been expecting someone old and wrinkled and was a little stunned at the youth and beauty of Jiwan.

When he lifted his head and very slowly moved his eyes in their direction, Manuela was transfixed by the swirling grey and violet storm that could be seen in them even from a distance.

"My father knows we are here," Hira said as they stepped back behind the boulder. Manuela had to pull Silvia away from the sight of Fritz. "Now we must prepare for Shatru. He is much stronger than the Rogs. The red twine that binds them is a draining string. Jiwan can do nothing to free himself or the others." Hira was squatting, her slim silver hands resting in her lap, her eyes down. "He cannot hold on much longer. Soon, it will be a life-draining string."

"But what can we do, Hira?" Manuela asked. She was peeling off the heavy grey outer clothing. "Silvia and I don't know any magic; we don't even know how to fight."

Silvia put her heavy things next to Manuela's and squatted down next to Hira. "But we want to help. Just tell us what to do," Silvia said with anger in her eyes. Manuela could see Silvia's determination and felt stronger. *Miss Sasha wouldn't have asked us to go on this journey if we weren't important for victory*, Manuela thought. *We've made it this far; we just need to hold on to each other until it's over.*

Hira looked up from her hands. Her slim pale face was so iridescent in the flickering shadows that when she looked at them, her large silvery-violet eyes seemed shocking in their intensity. "Don't you understand? Being human, you have the most power of all. We DragonFlies may hold the magic, Jiwan may be Keeper of the Hope that is necessary for goodness in the world, but it is only in humans that this hope, this goodness can be manifested." Hira tilted her head and her pink flossy hair wisped around in the crackling dry air. "The Rogs want to destroy the DragonFlies so that the humans will destroy each other."

Manuela blinked. She hadn't thought of it that way. She had almost forgotten about that other world, that world of SUVs and cell phones. She had forgotten about her mother and her father and her quiet neighborhood in Cleveland. *What if the ladies next door were mean instead of pleasant? What if the old man next door slashed her father's tires for driving off the driveway onto his lawn instead of letting him help fix it?*

Standing up with a graceful motion, Hira held her hand up and made some signals to the blue DragonFlies near her. They nodded and dispersed into the shadows with the other hiding DragonFlies. "Your desire to destroy the Rogs and free Jiwan and the others is the strongest magic that we have."

Suddenly the two Rogs stopped insulting each other and the cave was eerily silent. The dry burnt air began to stink with a rancid smell like an old unwashed dog. Hira stiffened and snuck around the boulder to take a look. The girls followed quietly.

The two ugly dwarfs were still there, standing as straight as their round forms would allow. But their attention wasn't on the odd group of captives on the dark blue disc. Manuela followed their gaze, (after painfully pulling her eyes away from Fritz), to the far end of the cavern where a network of tunnels opened up. She couldn't see anything there.

"What's …"

"Shhh," Hira said softly, putting her tiny finger to Manuela's lips. Manuela felt a tiny jolt with the contact and turned back towards the opening.

Chapter 28

Meeting Shatru

THEY BEGAN TO HEAR A THUMPING and then the openings began to swell with the disgusting forms of hundreds of Rogs. Covered with pussy bumps, their oozing black hides squelched and creaked as their large feet marched into the cavern. In the middle of the throng rose a much taller and larger figure. Manuela covered her mouth and grabbed Silvia's arm. Its large misshapen head was entirely covered in red eyes which darted in every direction with a lidless stare. Only on the very bottom of the head was a section without eyes, and this was a long fat-lipped mouth reaching from one side to the other. Between lips pale and scaly like a snake's belly, sharp uneven fangs stuck out randomly. But by far the most disturbing thing about what Manuela assumed was Shatru was his long oblong body covered with tentacle-like arms. They writhed when he walked like a clump of black worms trying blindly to escape from the fanged ball of eyes above it.

Manuela glanced at the disc and saw their friends shaking as the disc swung pendulum-like over the smelly pit. Fritz was whining and struggling weakly against the red twine. Jiwan was sitting up with his head held high. Manuela marveled again at how perfect he looked, even as he lay dying.

"RUNU, GOBAR, HAVE YOU OBTAINED THE FIRESTONE?" Shatru's loud gravelly voice rang out and filled the cavern.

"Not yet, my King, but I'm sure we are close," said the Rog who wouldn't throw the captives in the pit.

"I don't think they have it anymore, my King, and are just trying to stay alive by not telling us!" bellowed Runu.

"WHAT!" roared Shatru. "I TOLD YOU THAT THEY HAVE IT AND WE NEED TO GET IT. YOU DEFY MY BIDDING?"

"If it weren't for me," Gobar huffed, "he'd have thrown them down the pit, the idiot." Runu bared his teeth at the other Rog and hissed, covering his face in pink spittle.

"YOU WANT SOMETHING THROWN IN THE PIT, RUNU? SUNGUR, GADBAD, THROW HIM IN." Shatru's tentacles twisted and jerked and his slash of mouth twitched into a cruel smile.

Immediately, two of the ubiquitous Rogs with large dark mossy carapaces came forward and seized the suddenly submissive Runu.

"Don't do it, my King. I only want to obey! I ONLY WANT TO …" Runu's gurgling voice died off as they tossed him back violently into the smoky fumes.

The hall was silent. Manuela held her breath as she watched the swaying of the blue disc slowly stop. Jiwan was staring directly at the monster. His stormy eyes were filled with an intense light.

"So, Gobar," Shatru said a little less loudly. "Where is the firestone?"

"Well, you see …" Gobar began to cough and spit up a gob of phlegm. "I think if we eat all the others and chew on those wings of his then he might tell us where …"

"ENOUGH!" Shatru shouted. "You have failed. "Sungur, Gadbad, take his eyes and throw the rest down the pit."

Manuela and Silvia had to hide their faces in their hands as Gobar's pig-like squeals and screams rang out through the cave. Finally it was silent, and Manuela lowered her fingers. Shatru stood at the edge of the hole facing Jiwan. Almost all of his bloodshot eyes stared at the still magnificent golden DragonFly.

"Well, Jiwan. You still refuse to give up the Firestone. I don't know why. Obviously it hasn't helped you these last few days. Or are you secretly hoping that I will drop your companions there into the pit one by one?" Shatru's eyes dripped sweat onto the hot stones near the edge of the pit which sputtered and hissed with each drop.

"My friends know that it is not my decision that would take them there. The Firestone is too important to give up for one life." Jiwan's strong voice lifted off the disc in rich deep tones that belied his thin angled frame hunched up under the tight red ropes. "Besides, we both know that you will have us all eaten or thrown in anyway even if I do tell you where to find the Firestone." Jiwan smiled slowly and didn't show any fear.

"IDIOT FAIRY!" Shatru yelled so loudly that the echo bounced around the cavern and rattled the gravel. "TELL ME OR I WILL LEAVE NO ONE LEFT ALIVE!" Twitching madly, Shatru turned and addressed a particularly ugly grey-green Rog with red spines. "TELL THE TROOPS TO GET READY. THEY WILL GO ABOVE." The room was filled with snort-like gasps.

"EVEN IF NONE COME BACK ALIVE, THEY WILL HAVE SLAUGHTERED ENOUGH HUMANS TO CHANGE THINGS FOREVER."

Manuela tucked herself back behind the boulder, pulling Silvia with her. Hira turned sensing their confusion.

"Firestone? Why does *he* want this stone?" Silvia asked as if reading her thoughts. "Can they really go kill people?"

"The Firestone is the key to the hidden magic reserve that the DragonFly Keeper can use in an emergency. No one has ever had to use it, and no one has seen it. Although we believe it exists, it is almost a whispered myth among us anymore." Hira looked back at the troops of DragonFlies. "If we did have it, this war would be over. Whoever holds it can summon all the magic on earth and invest it any way they want. Once only." She shivered. "If Shatru gets it … well, you can imagine. Jiwan is using Shatru's desire to find the stone to stay alive. However, I believe Shatru is getting impatient." She pulled the girls back to their vantage point. "If we don't act soon, it will be too late." Shatru was conferring in a more quiet voice with some of his Rogs. "Indeed he can send them up to destroy mankind. Usually, the magic of the good would be strong enough to prevent such an onslaught of the non-magical world." She hung her head. "But since Jiwan's capture, he has been drained to almost nothing. And we need our Keeper."

Manuela's eyes watered and she clenched her hands into fists. Silvia's face was set in an angry frown. Suddenly Fritz jerked his head and looked in their direction. He strained against the red twine, barking.

"Get back!" Hira hissed as she pulled them back under the boulder's shadow. But it was too late.

As she heard the gravel crunch under Rog footsteps, Manuela saw a group of blue DragonFlies materialize out of the shadows and step forth holding their long lance-like swords across their chests. Then Hira gave a stern look and jumped up and turned the corner to face them head-on.

"Hira, you finally made it." Shatru's voice was less like a loudspeaker now. "I was wondering if you would be here for your father's funeral."

"You are wrong, Shatru," Hira said with her head held high, her hair flowing about her shoulders. "You know you are no match for the DragonFlies. Give us the captives and we will leave without killing you all."

The black squid-like arms stopped twitching and stretched out their full length. "Such attitude. Your father would be proud. If he weren't so shamfully tied up. Perhaps you would like to give me the Firestone. Then I just might give you the captives." Fritz barked and whined loudly. "Sungar, kill that stupid beast."

"Noooo!" Silvia cried as she jumped out and stood trembling next to Hira. Manuela's knees felt weak. She had to concentrate not to pee her pants. "Fritz has nothing to do with this. LET HIM GO!" Silvia wailed jumping up and down. The blue DragonFlies tensed and looked at Hira who was staring at Silvia with her mouth slightly parted. Finally, Manuela decided to get up and grab hold of Silvia.

"Silvia, stop. It's O.K.," she said as she grabbed onto her arms and held them.

"No it's not. It's not," sobbed Silvia, turning into Manuela's embrace. She was shivering but at least she had stopped jumping and seemed to look up as if finally realizing where she was.

Shatru's face showed undisguised smugness. "Are these the human warriors sent to defeat me? Is this what the

DragonFlies have been waiting for to bring down my downfall?" he laughed. Hira still held her head up high, but her cheeks were sallow and her wings were folded tightly against her back. "Get the dog, Sungar. Bring him to me."

Hira held Manuela's hand on one side with Silvia still huddled against Manuela as the sickening Rog tramped over to the disc and used a hook on a long pole to dig under some of the twine and lift Fritz up and over to the ledge. Fritz yelped and then stopped fidgeting. Sungar carried the panting Fritz toward Shatru. Silvia looked imploringly at Hira as Shatru's tongue flicked out and ran all along his white, veined lip.

Suddenly Hira tilted her head slightly and raised her violet eyes towards the high ceiling. There was a quick whistle and then a thump as Sungar took a step and then twisted on his ankle and fell. As he turned, the hook's sharp point cut through the twine and its red glow flicked out. Fritz didn't even hit the ground before he wriggled out and ran over to Silvia who bent and buried her face in his caramel-colored fur.

It took the Rogs a second to realize what happened, and by then Fritz was already nuzzling the two girls. Shatru's arms started waving frantically. "IDIOTS!" He hurried over to Sungar's body and stomped it to green ooze under his black toes. Turning to Jiwan, he screamed. "PREPARE TO DIE, BUG. I AM TIRED OF GAMES." Quickly he began marching back into the throng of Rogs, summoning various commanders with his many arms. Turning slightly he addressed Hira. "Firestone or not, I WILL kill you today."

Chapter 29

The girls fight the battle which decides it all

HIRA PULLED THE GIRLS BACK behind the boulder as dozens of blue DragonFlies, their wings outstretched, ran together and locked into a defensive formation. Red DragonFlies went aloft and intermingled with the blue ones to create a fast-moving shield which blurred into a pinwheel motion in the flickering smoky cavern.

"Girls, stay put unless a DragonFly tells you otherwise." Hira turned to take off and then paused. Turning back, she let her violet eyes turn soft and smiled. Holding out a long slim arm she touched each on the cheek in turn quickly and then was gone, flying up into the midst of the widening gyre above.

"What do we do?" Silvia asked looking around. She hadn't let go of Fritz, and was bent down hugging him.

"We stay put like Hira said."

"But we have to do something to help," Silvia said. While she understood that Hira wanted to protect them, she still felt like she should be doing something to help in the fight. While the DragonFlies were fierce and powerful, she had seen the sheer number of Rogs that swarmed down below them.

"Silvia." Manuela said with a whisper. She was staring at her sister. "Silvia, the Firestone."

"We don't have time to find it, Manu," Silvia said peering around the boulder. "It looks like Shatru is trying to drain the last of the Magic out of Jiwan." The blue disc was hard to see through the fighting, but Silvia could make out Shatru standing near the chasm and Jiwan's mouth clenched as his red twine harness glowed brighter than ever.

"Silvi, the Firestone," Manuela said again in a scratchy voice. Silvia turned, annoyed at her sister's insistence.

"I told you, we have to do something NOW to help ... what? WHY are you looking at me like that?" Silvia looked down at her chest where Manuela was staring. Somehow, when she had jumped out for Fritz, her Newari Gau Locket had bounced out of her jacket and dangled from its red velvet cord above Fritz's ears. The firelight made the tiny jewels glitter, especially the amethyst in the middle. She looked up and met Manuela's eyes. "You don't think ...? Could it be?"

"I think we should call Hira," Manuela said looking around for an available DragonFly. But no one was paying any attention to them. The air buzzed like mad chainsaws with only the deafening gurgling screams of the Rogs penetrating through. Fritz barked as Silvia stood up and started waving her arms around. But the DragonFlies were all busy.

"Let me help," Manuela said over the noise as she got to her feet. "They can't miss both of us together." The girls jumped up and down wildly and screamed Hira's name.

Finally an extraordinarily tall blue DragonFly seemed to materialize out of the blurry air in front of them.

"What are you doing!" he yelled.

"Hira ... the Firestone ... we need ..." Silvia said panting for breath.

The DragonFly frowned and made to take off.

"Wait!" Manuela reached out and grabbed him. He looked annoyed, but then his anger turned to astonishment and then excitement as he saw what Manuela was pointing at. Quickly he nodded and disappeared into the turmoil.

The girls turned and saw their friends huddled on the blue disc. *Maybe they won't make it,* she thought. Jiwan was slumped over, his golden hair spilling over his shoulders. The red twine glowed like a fiery snake around his legs, torso and arms. Silvia held onto the Gau Locket and rubbed it with her thumb. *Please let this work. That is my prayer. Do you hear that Miss Sasha?*

It was only a few moments but they seemed never to pass. Finally, Hira's billowy pink hair was in front of them, waving like a frothy sea at sunrise. Her face was set and her eyes glowed with a warrior intentness that heated her hair around her with static pops. Without hesitation she took a step forward and held the Locket in the palm of her hand.

"Where did you get this?" she demanded.

"Miss Sasha gave it to me before we began the journey." Silvia said meekly. "Hira, is this the Firestone?"

Without answering, she pulled it over Silvia's head, held it in front of her by its red velvet cord and closed her eyes. Silvia could see the gold and hand-set jewels glinting in the grey smoke. Suddenly Hira smiled and the amethyst began to glow faintly.

"We have won. The Firestone is not a myth after all. To think that humans have had it all this time." Hira lowered her hand and her smile faded. She nodded at the green DragonFly that had accompanied her and she flitted off. Turning to the girls she said in a serious voice, "You must listen to my instructions. We have only one chance to do this right. I need you to hold onto the Gau Locket with me. Then you need to close your eyes and repeat everything that I say."

"Hira, what is going to happen?" Manuela looked into the DragonFly's gentle yet dynamic face. Suddenly she felt an overwhelming sense of security. The small smile, the dewy sheen of Hira's skin, even in the middle of a battle, all pulled together to create such a strong feeling of peace, a sense of rightness. She felt herself let go and leap forward.

"What will happen, dear one, is that the DragonFlies will be filled with a power a hundred times that of what they have now. And with their combined energy from the Firestone, which we will unleash, a shield will grow and destroy anything evil for miles around." Hira held the Locket out with both hands and the girls reached up and grabbed hold.

When Hira closed her eyes, Silvia and Manuela did as well. Hira started mumbling in her strange tongue and they felt the Locket grow warm, then almost hot. Silvia could feel the tiny red garnets throbbing under her thumbs and dared not open her eyes. As Hira continued mumbling the noise of the battle began to subside. Suddenly Hira's voice became louder and she said clearly, "Ghaam jhulki sakyo. Polne ghaam chha." She repeated this clearly several times and then grew silent.

"Ghaam ... jhulki sakyo. Po ... Polne ghaam chha." Manuela began tentatively. All the practice they had with

236

the *shaanti* had paid off. "Ghaam jhulki sakyo. Polne ghaam chha," they began repeating after Hira, louder and louder. Suddenly, Hira gasped and they could feel her shaking as she held on to the Firestone. It was so hot now, Silvia couldn't even feel her fingers, but she didn't let go. Even without Hira's voice, they continued to yell, "GHAAM JHULKI SAKYO. POLNE GHAAM CHHA!" Inside Silvia's head she heard the whisper, "The sun is risen; the sun is hot."

The whole cavern seemed silent except for their chanting and the whisper going through her head. Then, without warning, Silvia was thrown back and she opened her eyes with a gasp as her breath left her. Above her a white light seemed to swell and explode without sound, only a whistling wind. In the instant that the entire cavern was aglow, Silvia saw hundreds of Rogs wither into dust and smoke. The red twine around Jiwan and the others dissolved away. But she also saw that Shatru was standing behind Hira, two black sticky tentacles twined around her neck and waist. Hira was hanging from them, her wings torn and hanging, dripping silver droplets onto Shatru's puss-oozing black hide. Her pink hair for once hung lifeless and tangled, and her skin was so transparent Silvia could see her heart just barely beating beneath her skin under her torn tunic.

Unable to move, Silvia screamed inside her head. The silence made her feel even more numb and helpless. Then Shatru dropped Hira and backed away as a glowing golden arrow pierced his many-eyed head. Grey blood gushed out as the golden arrow worked its way in deeper and deeper. Jiwan flew to Hira and the last thing Silvia saw before she blacked out was Shatru skittering away down a tunnel clutching the Gau Locket.

Meeting Jiwan

W HEN SILVIA LOOKED AROUND for Manuela, she saw her rushing toward Hira. Meeting her there, Silvia smoothed back stray pink strands from Hira's hot, pale face. Immediately, one of the white healing DragonFlies was kneeling beside Hira holding her wrists between her palms.

"Is she alright? Is she …" Silvia couldn't bring herself to even think it.

"She is alive. Barely." The white DragonFly had thickly curled black hair like the girls and it was twisted back at the nape of her neck with a blue cord. Now she undid the cord and her hair cascaded about her white robe. "I can only try this," she said as she took out a tiny glass vial of deep sapphire from a tiny cloth pouch attached to the cord. "It is very rare and reserved for drastic emergencies such as this." She began massaging lilac-scented oil into Hira's small temples. Hira stirred softly and opened her eyes.

"Oh!" Siliva started when she looked into Hira's eyes. They no longer held a stormy violet cloud but a pale lavender haze. Gone was the spark of power; instead Hira's pain poured out.

"Jiwan?" she asked in a dry whisper.

Silvia felt a warm presence and looked up before she heard him speak with his impossibly rich voice. "Hira, my daughter, I am here." Standing tall and absolutely beautiful, Jiwan nodded to Manuela and then Silvia. Silvia's breath caught in her throat when his large grey eyes peered deep into her. Then he bent down and motioned for the white DragonFly to back away, which she did graciously.

"Father?" Hira began but then she closed her eyes and clenched her teeth in pain.

"Hush. It will be alright, Hira." And Silvia believed him.

"But Father, I am dying. I can feel it." Hira's eyes let fall a few fragile tears that Jiwan wiped away gently with a finger. Manuela cast a worried look Silvia's way, but visibly relaxed when Silvia nodded her head and smiled and then looked back to Jiwan.

"You will not die today." Jiwan said softly as he bent down and kissed her on the forehead. There was an audible snap when his lips touched her feverish face. When he straightened up Silvia gasped again. Hira's eyes were no longer full of pain. Neither were they violet, but now a silvery steel that held the strength of mysterious power. But then Hira, now flush instead of pale, leaned up and grabbed her father's shoulders.

"Jiwan, NO!" she sobbed.

"Hush, now. I only have a moment left. Don't spoil what is meant to be, what is my right. Don't leave me with your tears." Jiwan was slumping over now and a blue DragonFly rushed to support him in his arms.

"What has happened?" Silvia asked, unable to stay quiet.

Hira's face grew solemn and then she smiled. "Jiwan has bequeathed the title of DragonFly Keeper, and his life, to me."

"So he is dying?" Manuela asked quietly. All of the DragonFlies seemed to have understood what was going on, and they knelt silently with their heads bowed and their arms outstretched amid the blood and gore.

"Yes, dear girls. I regret that I will not be able to better thank my saviors," he smiled and then grimaced as he laid back, his face ashen. "It is not only me, but the two of you who have saved Hira as well as myself today."

"But Sh ... *he* took the Firestone when he left. Even if all the Rogs have been destroyed, won't he now have all the power to create more?"

Hira shook her head with a faint faraway look in her eyes. She was holding both of Jiwan's hands in her own. "The Firestone is only a Gau locket now. It can only be used once. It no longer *is*."

Silvia sighed. When she saw Shatru scuttle off with the locket, she thought all was lost, and that they would have to hunt him all over again.

Hira stood, reluctantly letting go of Jiwan's hands. "Listen," she began in a different voice than she had ever before. "Jiwan has given me the ultimate gift of love, his life," she boomed out. "As your DragonFly Keeper, I ask that you honor him for his sacrifice for all our people and for all the world." As one, the masses of DragonFlies that could, stood up and opened their wings, some full, some tattered and dripping silver in the smoky gleam that wafted around the cavern since the Firestone's flash.

"Jiwan, as a people we salute you. Bravest and most honorable DragonFly Keeper to have ever lived." Hira knelt down beside him and bowed to the ground opening up her now healed and shining rainbow wings.

Manuela and Silvia bent closer to Jiwan and held onto his hands. His fingers were cold and fragile but they could feel the peace he held inside. He turned his eyes from Hira for a moment to them. They were light blue and fading fast. "Remember this if nothing else," he said cryptically. "If your love is strong enough to give to another, then you WILL have won. We will ALL have won here today." Silvia let her tears fall as she saw him quickly turn back to Hira and lock eyes with her. And then he closed his eyes and was gone.

Letting go of his hands, the girls sat back and snuggled Fritz between them. This moment was for Hira alone. She closed her eyes and leaned forward to kiss his cheek. A lone tear dropped onto his golden hair when she straightened up, but she did not tremble. Turning she nodded to two DragonFlies of a color the girls had never seen before. The two, dressed in a luminescent gauzy pearl-like fabric stepped forward and lifted Jiwan. They held his slender but long body high as all the DragonFlies closed their wings and placed their arms cross-wise on their chests, fists clenched. Then, with long silvery hair streaming behind them, they passed through the ranks of DragonFlies who stepped aside to let them pass.

Hira raised her hands and then clasped them together and bowed.

"They will take him to a secret resting place. It is our way." Hira said, placing a hand on Manuela's arm. Their other friends, the contacts, had mysteriously disappeared. The other DragonFlies began to mill about helping the wounded and gathering those who would never rise again. "We will have a feast in his honor when the time is right."

"Is it over?" Silvia asked looking around at the fallen DragonFlies and the mass of Rog gore. Now that her adrenaline was wearing off, the stench was starting to make her stomach turn.

"It is never over," Hira said softly, as she placed a palm on each girl's cheek. "But we have won for now. Peace and hope will flourish thanks to your bravery." She smiled and bent down to ruffle Fritz' fur when he snuggled into her. "And yours of course, brave Fritz."

Silvia could barely comprehend. They won. THEY WON! And they were all still alive! "WE WON! WE WON!" she cried jumping up and down, unable to contain her excitement. Manuela laughed and she and Hira started yelling too. Soon, all of the DragonFlies were letting out held-in tension in screams and yelps and songs of joy.

Chapter 31

The girls get some bowls

SILVIA RAN OUTSIDE. "Fritz! Fritz, where are you?" She ran down the sidewalk in the dark when she thought she felt rain. Stopping, she held out her hands and felt nothing. Then, as she started up again, she felt it: a few drops of rain and then some more splashing her cheek. She raised her face to the …

"Ahhh! Fritz!" Silvia wiped his saliva off her face as she sat up rubbing her eyes. Fritz backed up, his tongue wet and dripping. It was dark and quiet, but Silvia could sense right away that this was not the same place where she was when she fell asleep.

"Manu! Manu, wake up!" she said in a loud whisper shaking her sister.

"O.K.! O.K.! You don't have to kill me; I don't hibernate like you!" Manuela rolled over onto her back and sat up slowly. Silvia could just make out her dark curls jutting out around her pale oval face.

"Silvia? Where are we?" Manuela finally said in a tense voice.

"I don't know. All I remember was falling asleep in the Pine Tree Grove outside of Crystal Mountain after the feast." Silvia sighed remembering. After the DragonFlies had finished collecting their own, they had all marched unceremoniously back out through the tunnels. There they had huddled together and, whispering quiet words, they had all been whisked away to a beautiful grove of tall fragrant pines. The sun was warm and welcome as it dappled the soft needled ground underneath.

Hira had passed them off to a group of white DragonFlies again, and they had bathed and dressed in clean grey tunics, leggings and slippers. The DragonFlies were uncharacteristically talkative and happy, even braiding the girls' hair with white and gold threads and pinning it up. Perhaps they were *normally* this way and had only seemed solemn because of the serious situation they were in.

In any case, when everyone was clean, Manuela and Silvia followed the white DragonFlies to a wide clearing surrounded by the towering blue-green pines. Plates and mugs had been laid out in concentric circles for all of the DragonFlies, and for the girls. One particularly pale white DragonFly, with wispy blonde hair that floated to her knees, led them close to the center of the mandala of plates. There they had stayed until the sun set through the pine needles, feasting and laughing and finally getting to know the DragonFlies. She and Manuela had dropped right off to sleep when they were led through the dark to a pair of soft pine-needle mattresses.

But that's not where they were now.

"I think we're in a room," Silvia finally added. "Manu?"

"What?"

"I'm wearing a T-shirt and shorts."

"I am too."

"Manu?" Silvia was snuggled in close to her sister. "Manu, do you smell that?"

"It smells like Miss Sasha's house. Could we really …?" Manuela was cut off as Fritz pushed the door open with his nose and soft amber light flooded in from the hallway. If they were in Miss Sasha's house, they were in a room they had never been in before. Except for a long oak dresser along the wall, the room was bare of furniture. The walls were papered pale green with tiny pink flowers. Then Silvia saw what was laid out on the dresser.

"Manu!" she said jumping up. "Look at all these weird bowls! We must be in Miss Sasha's house!"

Fritz had been sitting in the hallway, panting and waiting. When he saw Silvia bolt out the door, he followed her.

"Silvia! Wait up for me!" Manuela said pushing back her hair from her eyes.

The hallway was short and soon they stood at the top of stairs carpeted with the same dull green carpet as the hallway. The strong appley-cinnamon smell of samudra was coming from down below. It was dark and quiet.

"Miss Sasha? Hello?" Silvia whispered as she started to tip-toe down the steps with Manuela and Fritz at her heels. "Miss Sasha? Ohhh!" Silvia almost fell as Miss Sasha's face peered at her from the darkness.

"Girls, are you hungry? I was just preparing a snack. You seemed so tired and hungry after chasing your dog." Miss Sasha, still wearing a plain brown dress with a dark purple shawl, crinkled up her nose and her eyes twinkled as she led them towards the kitchen.

Chasing our dog? Silvia mouthed to Manuela with a quizzical look. Manuela shrugged and they sat down at the same royal-blue marble-topped table. There in the corner a lamp was on, and the black and white tiled floor shone in its soft light. Gingerbread cookies with hot cinnamon buttons were arranged on a pale glass platter in the middle of the table.

"Are these samudra gingerbread men?" Silvia asked with a giggle.

"What dear? Oh, I haven't heard of that recipe. This is an old recipe passed down to me from my great Aunt Elaina." Miss Sasha shuffled over and placed a steaming mug of what looked like hot cocoa in front of each of them.

Silvia stopped giggling and looked sideways at Manuela. "Are you telling us you don't know what 'samudra' is?" She stared hard at the little old lady.

Miss Sasha's eyes crinkled again and she winked one of her pale blue eyes. "Is that some kind of fancy new thing the kids like nowadays? I'm a little behind the times." She sat down with a soft plop on a chair between the girls.

Manuela's mouth was open, but she put down the cookie she was just about to eat. Silvia's hazel eyes grew wide and wild. "What's going on?" she said shakily. "Miss Sasha, don't you want to ask us what happened? Don't you want to know about Jiwan and the DragonFlies?" Manuela stayed absolutely still as she watched Silvia start to get jittery in her seat.

"Is that some book you're reading, dear? Sounds good," Miss Sasha said smiling. She patted Silvia on the arm and then looked up at an old brass clock on a shelf above Silvia's head, avoiding her eyes. "Oh my, girls!" she said pushing herself up from the chair with a little effort. "It's really getting late. Your mother and father will wonder what happened to you. Hurry and drink your warm cocoa and have a fresh baked cookie. You'll feel much better, trust me," she said looking Silvia directly in the eyes finally. Her misty blue stare was impenetrable.

"I ... but ... you ..." Silvia began.

"Eat, eat. Trust me. Trust me, dear." Miss Sasha smoothed a stray strand of Silvia's long curls.

Sighing, Silvia picked up a cookie and started crunching. After a moment, Manuela, too, began nibbling and gave one to Fritz. After washing the cookie down with some cocoa, the girls got up awkwardly. Miss Sasha disappeared into the front room.

"Silvia, *I* remember what happened. It wasn't a dream" Manuela said firmly holding onto Silvia's arm.

"But, Manu? Why? Why would she just forget, or pretend to forget? Doesn't she want to know what happened?" Silvia gazed at the kitchen one last time before turning toward the door. "Did it happen? I mean, what do we have to show that it was true? Maybe it was just a weird shared dream."

"No, Silvi." Manuela let go of Silvia's arm. "*I* sure don't dream like that. Besides, I feel ... different. Peaceful. Don't you?"

"Yes. I guess I do."

Miss Sasha was waiting for them next to the table of bowls that had first mesmerized Silvia. She picked up a bright pink bowl the size of a cantaloupe and handed it to Silvia. "I think you should have this. It's wonderful to meet new friends and I would love another visit sometime. It gets a little lonely here all by myself." Silvia took the bowl with a sad smile. "And here's one for you, too," she said, handing Manuela a shallow green glass bowl with copper wires threaded through it.

The girls thanked her and shuffled out into the warm Cleveland night with Fritz. As the door clicked behind them, they stopped and stared at each other. Silvia felt muddled. It felt like they had been in there a long time but she knew it could have only been a half an hour or so. The moon was just rising in the sky.

Appendix
Language translations by culture

Nepali

This language is mostly spoken in Nepal and Bhutan, countries of Asia north of India. All of the names of the Rogs and DragonFlies are Nepali words. The DragonFlies speak Nepali. (The Rogs don't speak any known language.) *Samudra* and *Shaanti* are also Nepali words, although they are used in a fictional context in this book. Here is a list of translations in the order they appear in the book.

shaanti	peace
samudra	ocean/sea
Newari Gau locket	a small prayer box with verses stored inside
tala pahaad	book of the mountain
samaya	time
janataa	people
buddhi	wisdom
dhanyabaad	thanks
kripayaa	please

sudrabaar	friday
bayaa tira jaanos	turn left
dayaa tira jaanos	turn right
sidhaa jaanos	go straight ahead
bahini	younger sister
swaagat	welcome
namaste	goodbye/good morning
roknu	stop
yo mero galti ho	it is my fault
ghaam jhulki sakyo	the sun is risen
polne ghaam chha	the sun is hot

DragonFly Names:

Jiwan	life
Hira	diamond
Taaja	fresh
Jaado	cold
Sangeet	music

Rog Names:

Shatru	enemy
Sarpa	snake
Maarnu	to kill
Huri	storm
Dushta	wicked
Runu	to weep
Gobar	cow dung
Gadbad	confusion
Sungur	pig

Aymaran

This Native American language is ancient and spoken by over a million people in the Andes. It is an official language of Bolivia and Peru.

sajuna paqu, sara	blue gilded, I go away
ikiw puritu	I am with dream
kamisaraki	hello
kawkis unstanta	From where did you appear?
janiw yakti	I do not know

Latvian

Latvian is spoken mostly in Latvia, in northern Europe.

sapnis	dream
spane	sleep
labdien	hello, good afternoon

Italian

The native language of Italy, this language is spoken in many parts of South America and other parts of the world. There are many dialects, but one national language.

portami dentro la bocca del vulcano	take me inside the mouth of the volcano
volete un passaggio fino al vulcano?	Do you need a ride to the volcano?
si	yes
grazie	thank you
io	I
tutti fuori	everyone out
andiamo	let's go

Swahili

This Bantu language is spoken by some 80 million people all over East Africa and the Congo. It is the native language of the Swahili people.

kati ya usiku	in the middle of the night
kule	over there
mti mwanamke	tree woman
fanya haraka	hurry up

About the Author

TANYA PILUMELI has published poetry and done poetry workshops for children. This is her debut children's novel. She has taught English Literature at many universities and currently owns an Italian restaurant with her husband. She lives with her three small children, Giuseppe, Violetta and Dionisio and her husband, Alessandro in Geneva, Ohio. For more information, **and to order this book**, visit *tanyapilumeli.com*.